Knotty New Year

By Merri Bright

Knotty New Year

The Billionaire's Betasitter

Merri Bright

Bright and Dark Publishing

Editing by Aubergine Editing

Cover by Y'all That Graphic

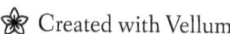 Created with Vellum

For Bekka and Courtney, for saying yes over and over again.
Such good girls.

Contents

Content Advisory

Thank you so much for reading *Knotty New Year*, the first book in my Billionaire's Betasitter world...even though it's listed second in the series.

Let me untangle this knot for you!

In 2022, I included a short story about Candy and Pax in the Omegaverse anthology, *Knotty or Nice*, hoping readers would like my first foray into M/F romance. They did! So I wrote Sunshine's Grump as the first full-length book, taking place three months after the short story.

When readers asked about Candy's story (no longer available), I decided to re-release it on its own. I ended up rewriting it instead, and turning that short insta-love story into a much longer, more heartfelt novel, still set the December *before* Sunshine's Grump.

No matter what order you read these standalone books in, I hope you love my take on sweet, funny, filthy M/F omegaverse romance.

The characters in this human Omegaverse romcom series are called betas (normal humans), omegas (typically women with soothing pheromones and ramped-up sex drives), and alphas (men and a few women who are assertive, respected, and attracted to omegas). Omegas and alphas together make up around ten percent of the population.

This "one-sausage special" has a lot of spicy ingredients, including, but not limited to: unique identifying scents, annual fertile heat cycles for the omegas, unusual peen, "make it fit" knotting, so much dirty talk, claiming, spanking, breeding, power imbalance, backdoor knotting, accidental pregnancy, and it is definitely only for adult readers.

Happy reading and have a very Knotty New Year!

Chapter 1

Candy

For my fifth birthday party, my mom baked five different kinds of miniature cupcakes. I got so excited I ate two of each, even the butterscotch lemon ones I hated, and spent the rest of the day sick to my stomach.

When I was eleven, I was so thrilled at being asked to the sixth-grade cotillion dance by Timothy Burgemeister Jr. and Samuel Maulding, I told both of them yes and had to do some tricky explaining to all the parents when the guys showed up with corsages.

I loved having choices more than anything.

But after I turned twenty, and everyone realized I wasn't just the only child of Marta and Elmer Kane, but also the first omega ever born to either family line? I lost all my choices, except one: which alpha I was going to pick.

At my hastily planned Designation Debutante Ball at the Omega League headquarters, I'd shocked everyone by *not* choosing, slipping out the kitchen door and back to my room alone instead. All the alphas at the party had been butterscotch lemons, as far as I was concerned.

Now, at twenty-four, even though my choices had grown even narrower, I'd decided to try one last time to have the life that had been snatched away from me in a burst of berry and cream perfume.

My teeth chattering from the late December cold, I stood with my finger on the doorbell of a colossal door to a Southern Gothic mansion that was easily five times the size of my parents' comfortable home. I was about to interview for a temp job working for Nicholas Paxson, the richest alpha on the East Coast. I wasn't certain what the job entailed exactly, but it didn't matter. This was my chance.

My choice.

I rubbed my sweaty hands on my thighs, doing a breathing exercise I'd learned online, which made my boobs almost pop one of the pearly buttons that were valiantly trying to contain the girls.

"Get back in there," I told my left boob, tucking it into the top. I eyed the right one with suspicion, too. But it was smaller, and usually minded its manners.

I had on one of my mom's "attorney outfits" for this interview. It almost fit me, though my curves made the skirt slightly too tight to bend over in. I'd decorated Mom's matching jacket with pastry crumbs and a clumsy splash of my cappuccino a half hour before, so I was only wearing the V-neck silk button-down blouse. The top was far too flimsy for the December chill, but I'd taken my puffy coat off and left it in the car to try and look professional.

The giant wrought iron gate had opened when I drove up, the guard quickly checking my license plate and waving my yellow VW Bug through right before he got in his truck and headed off. The second barrier, a line of tall metal bollards across the drive closer to the house, hadn't descended automatically for my car, though. I'd had to get out and walk through the cold, up the sweeping circular driveway. A few stray snowflakes swirled in the air now, making the scene almost magical.

Something about this whole thing felt too good to be true. But maybe I was due for some good luck?

The week before, my two besties, Soleil and Rain, had slapped together a website for a temp agency we were calling the Blue Skies Concierge Agency, along with a stack of printed business cards that looked official. On her way to St. Croix yesterday, Soleil had texted to say that a garbled phone message had been left about a last-minute position with Paxson Pharma. When I'd checked online, the only positions open were internships, and the PA spot for Nicholas Paxson himself.

So I'd decided to try for it. I was vaguely qualified to be a PA. Sort of. If you counted my unfinished degree and the subsequent two years of volunteer work in the Omega League's main office.

Still, the one thing that had been clear about the position they needed filled was the word "beta." I had spritzed on a significant amount of Paxson Pharma's own guaranteed scent blockers and hoped for the best. Maybe he would see how great I was at filing or social media updating, or whatever, before he smelled me. And then he might choose to let me stay.

A shiver of fear worked down my spine. What if Mr. Paxson thought I was an alpha chaser, like those women who hounded rich alphas all the time in the tabloids? What if he got one whiff of me and called the police?

"I can't go to prison. I look really, really bad in orange," I grumbled to the closed door. I yanked my finger away from the doorbell and took a step back, lifting my tan leather tote onto my shoulder.

Then I remembered. I couldn't go home. If I did, my parents would guilt trip me into marrying Andreas "Booger Nose" Vanderwall III, and I'd rather be homeless. Married to a weak alpha who constantly had a little booger trapped in his nose hairs, waving like a small white flag of surrender with every breath? Who smelled like mildew and tuna fish? Nope.

I had some blankets in the car. People lived in their cars, right? I could make a tiny nest out of the back seat...

I was just starting to back away when the giant door flew open, and I wobbled on my high heels, trying not to fall. An angry voice cut through the whistle of the bitter wind. "Get inside now. You're late, Miss Kane."

"I'm... late?" I blinked as a middle-aged, thin woman dressed in a navy-blue pantsuit bustled through the doorway and pulled me inside. I almost fell as she dragged me across a marble floor, my four-inch heels clacking.

"Yes, an hour late, and I may very well miss my flight with the storm that's coming," the woman complained. "I'm Mrs. Vincad, the house manager, and I do not have time to do the usual onboarding for a new employee."

I was already hired? I was giving myself a mental fist bump —the fluffed-up résumé I'd emailed must have been better than I thought—when she went on.

"Now, listen. The baby is upstairs sleeping. Here is the monitor." She thrust a white cylinder into my hand. "All the instructions are on the counter in the kitchen. The cook arrives at six every morning, and the maids at nine. You will stay out of their way, in the east wing. Do not ask the other staff to take care of him; they are not trained." She sucked at her teeth. "Do *not* ask Mr. Paxson to help with baby Benjamin. He's far too busy."

"Too busy for his own child?" I wondered aloud. I didn't even know the man had a child, and I'd researched him on the internet last night after Soleil's text. Though there really hadn't been much about his personal life, mainly just about his progressive work on omega health issues.

And what was Mrs. Vincad doing telling me all this? Gossiping about her boss was tacky. I'd opened my mouth to politely tell her so when she sighed.

"His nephew! Didn't the agency tell you? The baby is staying here through the holidays." Her lips curled into a tight smile. "Mr. Paxson will be working from home. He will spend time with Benjamin where he can, but he must not be disturbed while working. Just keep Benjamin quiet and out of the way. If you do, you'll get the extra bonus."

My mind spun. "Extra... bonus?"

"Yes, the ten thousand dollars. The holiday pay." Picking up a tablet from a nearby credenza, she opened a document. "Here is the NDA; please sign it now. It's standard," she grumbled as I attempted to read the impossibly tiny text.

I signed with my index finger on the tablet, fumbling as I tried to juggle it with the baby monitor. "The child, Mr. Paxson's nephew. Benjamin? He's here for how long?" It was unorthodox for a PA to do the sort of care she was asking for.

"Almost two weeks. While his mother and father are out of the country, until New Year's Day. It's Mr. Paxson's Christmas gift to his sister, Lindyann." She frowned, her dark eyebrows drawing together as she tapped away on the tablet.

I could hear the distant chords of a familiar lullaby from the plastic monitor in my hand. "I'm sorry, but... who exactly do you think I am?"

The woman's head snapped up, her watery blue eyes filling with suspicion. "You *are* from the Blue Skies Concierge Agency, yes? Theodore Sands set up the placement, at my request."

I forced a cool smile. "Blue Skies, yes. That's the agency that sent me here."

The woman's long nose seemed to get longer as she stared down at me. "You're very young."

"I'm twenty-four," I told her, "and if you've seen my résumé, you'll know that I have experience working with—"
She cut me off with a tsk.

"Yes, yes, I'm sure you're a very acceptable betasitter." She checked the tablet again. "Right, Mr. Paxson's PA now has the NDA. He already has your details. You have your instructions. I have to be at the airport in thirty minutes, so I'll leave you here—"

I skidded to a stop as her words registered. "Wait, a *betasitter*?" My voice sounded like a rubber duck being stepped on. "I'm here for the PA spot, I think? For Mr. Paxson."

"Oh... no." Her face went pale. "The PA spot was filled last week, by Mr. Sands. The one who called on behalf of Mr. Paxson yesterday. You're the nanny. Well, the replacement nanny." She stared down at her tablet again, then back at me, looking like she was about to faint, so I reached out to grab her arm. "Oh god, you haven't had the background checks run. You don't have a degree in childcare. If you're not a betasitter, I can't *leave*."

"I'm so sorry," I gasped, as the severe woman began crying.

"It's my mother. She's in the hospital in Madrid..."

The corners of my lips trembled in sympathy. "Well, you're going to make it. You're going to see her for Christmas," I said firmly. "And don't worry. I have years of experience with children. My résumé for betasitting is even more extensive than my office work." It was true; back when everyone had thought I was a beta, I'd had constant requests to betasit for the families in our upscale neighborhood. It was only after I perfumed as an omega that the requests stopped. No one wanted an unattached omega in their homes, tempting their menfolk with wicked wiles and sexy smells.

"I can't," she said, her tone thick with pain and resignation. "I'll have to call my family and let them know."

Before I could think better, I did something truly shameful. I placed my hand gently on top of hers and sent a wave of what I called my "omega whammy" in her direction. "No, Mrs. Vincad. Go to your mother. I promise, I have this under control."

Alphas had a forceful, powerful pheromone that could make grown-ass adults pee their pants. They could growl and bark and do all sorts of things to get their way. Omegas had the same skill, but expressed differently. We could soothe and calm with a touch and a word.

It came in handy when omegas got pulled over for speeding. Not that I had ever used it that way more than once. Or twice.

"Are you sure?" Her gaze skated over my outfit, like she could tell I was dressed in my mom's work clothes. "What's that delicious smell?"

I wiped some crumbs off my top, laughing nervously. *Crap.* Using my omega whammy had overwhelmed the blockers, making my scent leak a bit. "A little of my breakfast custard tart, I'd imagine. So sorry." I nodded briskly, competently, adult-ly, when Mrs. Vincad's eyes narrowed. So I sent another wave of my mojo at her. Her eyes went slightly cloudy. *Oof. Maybe too much.* "You can call Blue Skies now and ask them to send over my childcare résumé." My nonexistent one. I lifted an eyebrow, trying to imitate the expression my friend Rain called "Let Me Talk to Your Manager." It worked.

In ten minutes, I was alone in a massive kitchen with a monitor in one hand and a manual that read more like a contract than babysitting instructions. Hearing some cooing on the tiny speaker, I dropped it into my enormous purse, filled with everything I could possibly need for a long weekend, other than a change of clothes. But I was set if I got stranded in an airport, or in case of a sudden zombie apocalypse. My friends could laugh at me, but I'd told them my preparedness would be why we survived. I probably had enough candy and energy bars in there for a month.

"Upstairs, she said," I muttered, rounding a corner to where I assumed the stairs would be. "But which stairs?" I scanned my surroundings, humming the Christmas song that had been playing on the radio on my way over. "Okay, Candy, if you were a nursery, where would you be?"

"What the hell are you doing here?" A deep voice had me looking up. And up.

And up.

Standing not three feet in front of me was Nicholas Paxson. Six foot, seven inches of muscles and power, wrapped in navy dress trousers and a crisp white shirt, undone at the collar. The open buttons revealed a triangle of tanned skin that for some reason I wanted to lick more than any ice cream cone I'd ever held in my life.

"I bet you taste like chocolate," I whispered.

He made a low, strange growling sound, like a motor had started up in his chest. I blinked. Was he purring?

A wave of... *something* washed over me—heat? Lust?—and I felt my knees go dangerously weak.

He had mahogany hair that was sculpted into a wave over his forehead, and the tiniest bit of salt and pepper at his temples. His cheeks above the trimmed, dark beard were tanned, as if he spent most of his time outside or on a boat, and his deep brown eyes had lines at the corners. His suit was cut perfectly, but the body beneath it was too muscular to be concealed, and I could see his thighs flex as he shifted his weight.

Fuck. He looked like the cover model of every Daddy-dom book I'd ever read, all rolled into one. But bigger, harder, and... angrier.

He wasn't purring now.

"Who are you?" he demanded. His lip curled into a sneer that made me want to apologize, drop to my knees, and promise to be a good girl.

I took a shaky breath and exhaled on a whimper as his scent rushed over me. It was pine and... thunderstorms? I inhaled deeply, letting my eyelids close the smallest bit. Tasting it on the back of my tongue.

He stepped even closer, and my core honest-to-goodness clenched as he loomed over me. "Who. Are. You?" he repeated, his nostrils flaring.

"Y-y-you—your..." I tried to make the words, "Your sitter," emerge, but I was breathing so fast, I thought I might pass out. All that came out was, "Your s—" and when he stepped even closer, baring his teeth, I leaned back, my heel catching the edge of the rug. I started to fall.

Iron bars wrapped in a silk suit tightened almost cruelly around my waist.

He snarled, and my pussy did that clenching thing again, but this time, I could smell my own berries and cream omega perfume. "Mine?" he demanded.

I nodded, shook my head, then nodded again. His eyes narrowed. "Not... yours... I meant," I said, relaxing into the harsh grip, though I knew I should be trying to stand on my own. "I'm your..." At that instant, a baby's wail emerged from the monitor in my purse. "Your sitter," I finished. "Your betasitter."

Chapter 2

Pax

I f I didn't know fairy tales weren't real, I would have thought the woman melting in my arms was a princess, spun from some unknown bright magic.

Or a succubus, formed from my darkest desires and sent from Hell to tempt me.

Or an angel, untouchable and perfect. Forbidden.

I scoffed internally at my ridiculous, unfamiliar romantic thoughts.

Her hair was a tumble of dark waves that made my hands itch to weave through them and tug until she whimpered. Her eyes were deep pools of whiskey and chocolate that fluttered shut as I leaned over her. Her mouth formed a small O when I tightened my grip on her plush curves, her cheeks going pink as her blossoming scent revealed exactly how much she liked the sudden bite of my fingers in her softness.

I wanted to bite more than that, I realized, staring at the pulse that thudded at the base of her graceful neck. When she'd stuttered, I'd heard her answer my demand with a faint,

"I'm yours," and my dark, possessive heart had roared a *yes!* My teeth ached to bury themselves in her, taste her. Mark her.

Claim her for mine, forever. And then strip her bare and teach her exactly what that meant.

What was happening to me? I'd never reacted like this to *any* woman.

I'd almost fucking bitten a stranger. A girl.

In no universe was the soft omega in my arms the betasitter my previous PA had hired for the rest of December. I'd approved that one's résumé and done a tele-interview. She was sixty-eight, Croatian, had a doctorate in early childhood education, and had raised three of her own to adulthood.

This little omega, who smelled like strawberries and fresh cream, and whose skin promised to taste the same way, was practically a child herself. Curvy and young and a temptation I had no business handling. Not that my cock cared one damned bit. I hadn't been this hard since my first rut, back when I was eighteen... which was twenty years ago. *Shit.* Twenty-one. I was thirty-nine now.

Thirty-nine years old, and I would bet all three billion dollars of my own investments, and the whole of Paxson Pharmaceutical Enterprises, that I had just met my true mate.

My omega soulmate.

My stomach did a slow somersault. This girl might not even be as old as my youngest sister. What if she was a teenager? She looked like one, dressed in an older woman's ill-fitting clothes. Thank fuck my nephew had let out that short cry when he had, or I might have lost control and bitten her anyway.

As soon as she regained her balance, I let her go. "How old are you?" I demanded, and winced. I hadn't meant to ask that. I was going to ask her name.

Her dark eyelashes fluttered shut, and I took the chance to

adjust myself discreetly, grabbing my phone and tapping out a quick message to my new PA, Theodore.

"I'm twenty-four," she answered.

A dark inner voice roared. *Old enough. Claim her!*

I didn't look up from my phone, waiting for an answering text while I fought for control. "And who are you?"

"My name is Candy. I mean, Candace. Candace Kane."

I choked out a laugh. "Candy Kane? Try again, sweetheart. If you're going to lie, make it believable."

She crossed her arms over her chest, plumping up two of the most luscious breasts I'd ever felt guilty looking at. "I'm not lying. I'm Candy Kane. My birthday is December twenty-fourth, and my parents have terrible taste." She mumbled low, "It's not like I'd *choose* to have a stripper name."

I kept my eyes on my phone, but lifted one eyebrow as I typed. "Good girls don't tell lies, little Candy. That may be your name, but you haven't been truthful. I'll give you one more chance."

"Or what?" she said breathlessly, and the air between us filled with the most decadent perfume, making me almost groan aloud.

"Wahhhhh!" My nephew let out another cry, this time in earnest, and she spun on her heel—almost toppling over again—and crossed to the stairs.

"Where do you think you're going?"

"You may not want me as your betasitter, but someone needs to take care of that baby, Mr. Paxson." I watched her stride away from me, her plump ass in that too-tight skirt moving like a fucking snake-charmer.

My phone vibrated, and I spent the next two minutes cursing fate, my house manager, and omegas everywhere. I read my PA's texts and quickly dialed his number. "Theodore? What do you mean, there aren't any betasitters to be had? I have three billion dollars. I can afford to pay *Santa* to come down from the goddamned North Pole and watch this kid."

Theodore sputtered something about a storm of the century and closed highways. "Mr. Paxson, it's only days before Christmas, and your home is rather isolated. They're expecting gale force winds, and at least ten feet of snow. It's a historic blizzard."

"*Five* days before Christmas," I snapped back, then paced to a window and looked out. It was snowing hard. And it had been cold enough this week for the snow to stick as it came down, though the wind was blowing the whole world white. I had a four-wheel drive truck, but it would be taking my life in my hands to go out in it. And I couldn't leave Benjamin with an unknown woman.

I was stuck here, with the one omega on the planet I didn't know if I could resist.

"Call every agency you can, Theodore. This is your first real test as my PA. Don't let me down." He sighed, and I pulled the curtain shut as I hung up on him. Before I could put my phone away, it buzzed again. "Lindyann, this was the worst idea you've ever had," I said by way of greeting.

"It's lovely to hear your sweet voice as well, dear brother of mine," my twenty-four-year-old sister snarked back. Twenty-four years old, the same age as the forbidden omega upstairs.

I had been more of a father to Lin and the rest of our siblings after our parents' deaths over fifteen years before. Our youngest sister was still in high school, but she and most of the rest of the family were in Colorado, skiing for the school break. I was supposed to join them with the baby in the New Year, and hand him back to his parents when they returned home.

"How's my Little Ben?"

I sneered at the receiver. Her husband had taken to calling himself Big Ben and the baby Little Ben, like it was some sort of clever play on words. I wasn't going to encourage it. "Come back and get the baby, Lin," I demanded. "The nanny didn't show."

The line squawked—with laughter. "Hire another one, Daddy Warbucks."

"There aren't any more. There's a snowstorm, and my new PA is *useless*." I almost mentioned Candace, but I knew my sister would go nuts, possibly start planning a wedding. I had never had an omega in my home. I had no interest in romantic entanglements, and just had a few discreet friends who were happy to join me in anonymous hotel rooms when my body reminded me it existed.

Lin started blabbering about how gorgeous it was in Costa Rica, and how I should honeymoon there someday. "It's a perfect place to bring children when they're older, too," she said. I rolled my eyes as she went on about the national parks and the wildlife.

The whole reason she had saddled me with my nephew was, in her words, "to remind me how wonderful babies are." She mistakenly believed caring for her son would kick-start my alpha impulses to breed my own children. I'd told her raising my nine younger siblings for a decade and a half had fully quenched those desires.

I sucked in a breath, and the flavor of strawberries and cream lingered on the back of my tongue. For a split second, I imagined fucking that sweet little omega who was upstairs right now, hearing her cry out with pleasure as I worked my knot into her, filling her until she was swollen with my seed and pregnant with my child.

My cock jerked again, so hard my knot began swelling in my trousers, like a damned teenager.

"...the whole purpose was for you to get to know him. And you spend too much time working. Nicky, I left enough diapers to last through the Apocalypse, and enough formula and food for a hundred babies. You managed to keep all of us alive after Mom and Dad died. I'm sure you can handle a week or two on your own. But, if you really can't, maybe we can get flights back..."

She sounded stressed, which wasn't fair. I'd agreed months ago to keep the baby. Lin was an omega, and Ben was her true mate, which meant she was probably fated to have seventeen babies before she was done. Watching this one before her life turned into a carnival of diapers and nighttime feedings was the least I could do.

"Forget it, Lin. You're right, I can handle diapers for a little while. Have your dream vacation. The real nightmare's only beginning, you know."

She just laughed. "When you meet your perfect match like I did, you'll want your own. You won't be able to resist. Trust me, all it took was one breath of Big Ben's scent and I—"

"Ah! Stop talking," I shouted into the phone. "I never want to hear about that man's scent again." Her giggles had me smiling. "And we can't all be as lucky as you and Ben Senior. Not all of us get the fairy tale."

I blinked at my own words. Fairy tale. Princess. Strawberries.

My hand still smelled like her.

"Mom and Dad were true mates," she insisted. "And I found Ben. Your mate is out there somewhere. I know she is."

No, she was in *here*. Inside my fucking house, right now. Still, I hedged. "You know a lot of people don't even believe in true mates anymore, Lin."

We both went quiet. Our brother Victor had met his true mate the year before, at her wedding to another alpha, a friend of Victor's from university. Victor had changed since, and not for the better. He'd cried on my shoulder for days, insisting he could still smell her on his skin after embracing her at the reception. He'd dropped out of our weekly family calls, then left the country, telling us he'd come back when he could be sure he wouldn't go feral, track his true mate down, and kill her husband.

I'd hired a private investigator to find him, so I knew he'd traveled to Chile recently, and was alive. But not much more than that.

I held my own hand to my nose and inhaled deeply. Strawberries and cream, so strong she could be in the room with me. His mate couldn't have smelled nearly as good as this little omega...

Damnit. This little, far too young, innocent omega.

"Nicky, are you still there? I can come back if you really need me."

"Don't worry about Benjamin," I said gently, trying to ignore the hammering of my heart, and the pervasive aroma of ripe summer fruit that had my feet itching to race upstairs. "I'll keep him alive until you get back to the States. Be safe. I love you."

"I love you, too, Nicky. You're the best big brother I have."

"I'm going to tell the others you said that," I warned.

"Go ahead. Just remember, I chose you to watch Little Ben for a reason."

"Yeah, free childcare," I teased.

"No, because there's no one else in the world I trust more with my baby. Not even our other brothers." Her voice went a little raspy. "Have you heard from Victor?"

"I haven't found him. But I'll keep trying. Now don't worry about Ben."

When she hung up, I ignored the impulse to sneak back upstairs and spy on Candy. Instead, I opened my laptop and did some investigating to find out what had happened to the original betasitter.

Then I sent flowers to the hospital where she was apparently recovering from a concussion and broken collarbone that she'd sustained when her car slid on an icy bridge the day before.

Finally, once I'd texted all the information I could find on Candace Kane to Estefan Morales—the private investigator I'd hired to find Victor—and instructed Theodore to call off the nanny search, I let myself do what I'd wanted all day long.

I went to spy on the trick fate had played on me. My own true mate, here in my home. So close... and yet untouchable. Far too young, too enticing, too naive, for someone like me.

Chapter 3

Candy

I had never felt so unprepared for anything in my life. I'd walked up to this house hoping to weasel my way into a job I was only nominally qualified for. Instead, I found it a struggle not to run back downstairs and throw myself in the arms of an alpha who had no interest in me whatsoever.

I'd lost my mind.

"Now, Benjamin," I said to the baby who was standing inside his crib, tears glistening in his huge chocolate-brown eyes as he stared at me without blinking. The crying had stopped the instant I entered the room, and he seemed fascinated by me for the moment.

He looked to be about eleven months old, but the intelligence in his expression and the words he'd babbled at me when I entered seemed much more advanced. He was also one of the cutest babies I'd ever seen, with a tiny lick of dark hair that stood straight up like an Oompa-Loompa.

"I'm your betasitter, sweet boy. My name is Candy Kane. And no, before you ask, I am not one of Santa's elves. I'm sorry it took me so long to get to you. But what kind of house has twelve bedrooms? Entire wings of them?"

I fumbled in my purse for the manual Mrs. Vincad had given me, scanning the instructions. There was a list of foods he was and was not supposed to eat, directions to give him formula at certain times and with meals, and very firm instructions not to allow him too much screen time. I snorted; I'd seen plenty of documents like this before. Maybe not quite as many subsections on "stimulating classical music" as this one, but at least the little guy had no known allergies.

"If it keeps you alive and not screaming, I'll let you watch the director's cut of *Lord of the Rings*, kid."

Still standing behind the rail of his crib, he let out a strange half-snort at that. I rummaged in my purse for my phone, to check if I had any classical music in a playlist. I'd just pulled out my car keys and a squishy strawberry plushie Rain had given me for my birthday when my phone pinged, and Benjamin fussed. He had his fist out grasping for the toy, so I handed it to him and quickly checked my texts. It was Rain, asking about the job. I was just texting her to tell her I was busy, when I heard an odd, muffled sound.

Benjamin was foaming at the mouth. No, not foaming. I grabbed the toy and realized the baby had somehow bitten through the fabric and now had a mouthful of the tiny foam pellets that filled the center of the toy.

"Snickerdoodles!" I yelled, picking him up and running my finger through his mouth, trying to remove all the tiny white foam balls. "Come on, Benny." He opened his mouth, and I saw more at the back of his throat. I swept my finger across his tongue again, desperate to get the last of the little pellets. Brought on by the sudden stress, the nursery room filled with the scent of burned cream tarts and scorched berries. *Crap.* It was too cold to open a window and air out the room...

I had a sudden, terrible vision of the baby choking and me in handcuffs, explaining to the police that I wasn't really a beta-sitter. I was an omega who'd entered the house under false pretenses. I stuck my finger back into Benjamin's mouth, who bit down.

"Ow! Son of a butterscotch biscuit, kid!"

"What did you just say, omega?"

The abrupt question startled me so much that I almost dropped the baby. The alpha was there before my first high-heeled wobble had even begun, grabbing Benjamin and glaring at me. His expression as he quickly settled the baby—who was now babbling happily—in some sort of bouncing swing, said he knew I was hiding something. I dropped my gaze, tears pricking the corners of my eyes, and... saw his trousers.

Tented out, his dick straining against the fabric.

My eyes shot back up to his face, which had gone slightly ruddy as he scowled down at me. "Did you just yell... snicker-doodles?" he demanded. I sucked in a breath to answer, and my lungs filled with pine and thunderstorms again.

And my underwear filled with slick.

Goddamnit. My panties were not up to this sort of onslaught. I was going to leak down my damned legs if I didn't stop breathing in his potent man musk.

His eyebrows met in the center and dipped low. "Potent man musk?"

I'd said that out loud? "Absolutely not, sir. I would never comment on the scent of my employer, sir." I slapped a hand over my own mouth to stop the words from flowing out.

But he'd shuddered when I said sir.

Wait. Had he really? I clenched my thighs as his nostrils flared wide. "About what you're probably smelling now, sir..." He flinched at the word this time, and I could see his cock jump, even through his trousers. "Sir," I repeated breathily, as a sort of experiment. I reached for the broken stuffie. "I am so sorry. I gave the baby this toy and he—"

His scowl went hard, and suddenly, the game was over. "You don't give a baby this age a toy not rated for under three years old," he muttered. "You're *obviously* not a beta, or a sitter at all, are you?" He sneered, his dark eyes cold as the snowstorm outside. "You're still a child yourself."

I didn't say anything. I had a terrible habit of bursting into tears when people were upset with me, and he wasn't just upset. He was enraged.

"Well, *answer* me. Are you a sitter? Or an imposter?"

I jutted my chin out slightly to keep the tears from falling, a trick Soleil had taught me at an abysmal Alpha-Omega Meet-and-Greet two years before. Back then, I'd been crying because aggressive alphas were surrounding me and wouldn't let me leave. Now, an alpha couldn't get rid of me fast enough.

After a few seconds, I managed to say, "I'll just... go."

Benjamin started fussing, and Mr. Paxson made a sound of disgust as he turned away from me and went to take care of his nephew. I fished my car keys out of my purse and fled, trying not to trip as I descended the stairs. The front door was heavy, but when I opened it, I could hardly see the pavement that led to the bollards where I'd parked. Snow was swirling into the house, and I threw myself through the door and closed it behind me, my eyelashes practically caked with snow in an instant.

I couldn't drive in this. But I wasn't welcome to stay.

I struggled toward the car, making a plan. I'd turn the heater on, and I had energy bars and a bottle of water in my purse, as well as some mints and half a croissant from breakfast. If the snow stopped, I could drive to Soleil's... No, her entire family was away for the holidays. Rain lived much farther, in a sketchy neighborhood, but I was always welcome there. I tried to remember how much gas I had... and then I blinked, rubbing my eyes to even find my car. The snow was blinding me. I stumbled on my stupid shoes and fell onto a patch of crinkly, frozen grass.

When I rose, I was even more turned around. I wandered in the white-out until my toes and fingers started to lose sensation. My hair whipped around my face along with the snow, making it impossible to get my bearings.

Oh, god. This was how I died. Alone, in a freak snowstorm.

I screamed at the sky, shaking my numb fist. "It's not fair!" The wind slapped my face, and I fell back... into warmth.

"Life isn't, princess. You'll learn that when you're older," a very comfy, muscular pine tree growled into my ear as he lifted me off the ground. I burrowed my face into his warm, hard chest as he carried me back inside, my legs over one arm, my back supported by the other.

He stopped just inside the door, but didn't set me down. He was shaking. Shivering?

"If I hadn't heard the door slam," he snapped. "If I'd gone to the back of the fucking house, to the kitchen. If I hadn't *been* there." He pulled his face back, and I realized he was trembling with rage. "You. Could. Have. Died!" He started shaking me on each word, but he didn't set me down. He held me even closer, his face buried in my damp hair.

"I'm... I'm sorry," I said, reaching out with a wind-reddened hand to cup his cheek. His beard was short, and the snowflakes that had been caught in it were already melting. "I thought you wanted me to leave."

He let out a breath. "I did. I do. I don't want you here. But I'm not going to let you die out there." My heart felt like a crumpled tin can, getting squashed a little more with each word.

"Where's the baby?" I asked.

"Safer than you were. He's buckled in his play chair."

"That's good." My teeth had almost stopped chattering. The alpha set me down, and I wrapped my arms around the silk shell that was now completely transparent, and soaked through. The movement made my breasts pop up, right under my chin, practically. His eyes fixed on them, and I knew that Mr. Nicholas Paxson might not want me here.

But he wanted *me*.

And for the first time in my entire life, I felt the sort of desire that everyone always went on about, when they whispered about omegas. The melting, all-encompassing lust that thundered like a runaway train through my entire body, changing the landscape of what I had previously thought would be sufficient.

No touch would ever be enough if it didn't come from the hands of Nicholas Paxson. But I wasn't going to turn into the sort of caricatured alpha-chasing omega the movies and books all showed. The kind he probably thought I was, showing up here, claiming to be a betasitter. I knew he didn't return my feelings; he was already muttering about how short-sighted and immature I was.

So I straightened, pulling away from him a step. "I'm sorry, Mr. Paxson. I didn't mean to inconvenience you." I waited for his eyes to move from my pink nipples that were trying to stab their way through the wet silk to get to him. I had a feeling I was going to be waiting a long while; he was staring at my breasts, his brow furrowed and eyes slightly narrowed, like he was very disappointed in them and wanted to teach them a lesson. I jutted my chest out even more as I inhaled. "Is there somewhere I can dry off?"

"My room," he said absently, eyes boring invisible holes in my top.

He was taking me to his room? Had he changed his mind

already about wanting me here? I'd never imagined my nipples had magical powers, but they'd mesmerized this alpha. Mammary mind-control was apparently a thing. Good to know.

"Your room?" I breathed. His eyes were burning, jet-black coals, and when his tongue traced his lower lip slowly, I gasped slightly, causing one of the pearly buttons of my top to pop out of the buttonhole. I reached up to re-fasten it.

It was like a spell had been broken. He ran a hand over his beard, muttering something about going to jail or Hell, and then pivoted, his snow-covered dress shoes squeaking on the marble. He was a few yards away when he barked out, without turning his head, "Well? Are you coming or not?"

"Yes, sir," I squeaked, following him as fast as I could up the winding stairs. We turned down a hallway I hadn't seen before. It smelled more like Mr. Paxson here, though I could pick out a few other scents. Housekeepers, maybe? But mostly, it was him. The double doors at the end of the hall had to lead into a big bedroom. His bed.

My pussy gave the best imitation of a fist pump she could, more of a flutter, and the air around me began to smell like baking tarts. My vaj was completely on board with this unexpected turn of events.

"I'm drying off in your room?" That seemed unlikely. I was getting wetter by the second.

"Fuck no," he said, stopping abruptly. He changed directions, heading back down the hall.

Wait. He *had* been taking me to his bedroom. He absolutely had.

He led me to a different doorway, then looked down at my enormous purse. "That's not a suitcase." I frowned in confusion, but he went on before I could answer. "You need to change. You'll probably fit into Lin's clothes."

Lin? I sucked in a breath and realized the door he'd stopped in front of, the one to the left, smelled of another woman. Another omega. And when he opened the door, the scent of lemons flooded out to greet me.

My employer's dark eyes raked my form. "Take a hot shower. She's not as curvy as you, but you'll find something. She leaves clothes here for her visits."

"Lin's *visits*?" I was still in the hallway, but my feet would not move. A strange sound started up in my chest. I pressed a hand to my sternum, wondering what was happening.

But I knew. I was embarrassed and ashamed—this alpha did not want me; he'd already said that very clearly—but the sound I was making for the first time in my life was an omega growl.

I'd only heard it once before, in a documentary my class at the Omega League had watched together. It had explained some of the less commonly known facets of being an omega, although we'd all learned the basics in our general sex education classes in high school. Most omegas started perfuming around eighteen. I hadn't until I was twenty, starting my junior year at college. I'd been the oldest in my Omega League beginning classes, but we'd all watched the movie with a mixture of fascination and horror.

Omegas were generally believed to be more passive, emotionally fragile, insert-whatever-patriarchal-bullshit-here, as long as it resulted in omegas not being given fully equal opportunities. Society at large saw alphas as titans of industry and pillars of strength, both physically and societally. Omegas were cast as the opposite: unable to control ourselves, just as we couldn't control our perfuming around compatible alphas. And the omega growl would happen when an omega felt an alpha belonged to her. It was a way of marking one's territory.

Though I'd never growled before. My omega response was

usually just spontaneous crying, as if being an omega meant your tears ducts were the part that had to be wide enough to take a knot. I had mostly cried rage tears in my four years of living the curse.

I fought to control the feral sound that was rumbling in my chest right now, hyper-aware of the amused regard of the alpha I was metaphorically pissing on. "Lin?" I repeated, trying to cover up the sound with a cough. "Your girlfriend?"

The edge of his lips twitched, like he was suppressing a smile. "Lindyann, Benjamin's mother. She's my sister, little girl. One of many."

"I'm not a little girl," I muttered as he pushed the door open. He waved me inside, and I saw that the room had obviously been decorated by a teenager at least a decade ago, complete with old soccer trophies, K-Pop boy band posters, and a hideous, homemade pink and purple quilt topping the queen-sized bed.

"You're the same age as my sister." He leaned closer to me, and I could taste his pine and storm scent on the back of my throat. His voice scraped against my neck, and I shivered at his flashing, nearly bitter-chocolate eyes. "I raised her, and our younger siblings as well."

"You... raised them?" My heart thudded painfully at the realization that this alpha wasn't just dominant and drop-dead gorgeous. He also had a tragic backstory. Fuck, how was I supposed to stop perfuming around this omega-trap?

"I did. Hell, I changed my youngest sister's diapers, little omega. Now run along and get dried off and dressed." His lips curled up. "Or do you need me to change you?"

I blinked. He blinked too, the tops of his bronze cheeks going the tiniest bit flushed. Like he couldn't believe what he'd just said.

I could believe it, and it did a great job of pissing me off. It was just more of the same shit, if you asked me. Omegas were always treated this way, no matter their age.

I ran a tongue over my lower lip, slowly, then bit it, every bit as slowly, smirking internally at the fact that this alpha, who was trying to treat me like a child, now hadn't blinked in over a minute. I sucked in a sharp breath, and his eyes fell to my boobs once more.

"Diapers are your thing, then? Age play isn't one of my kinks," I managed to say, then inhaled deeply, loving the slow slide of his Adam's apple under his short beard as he stared at my tight nipples beneath the silk. "But I won't shame you. A man of your advanced age probably needs whatever help he can muster to get the old juices flowing, am I right?"

Before he could answer, I slammed the door in his face, slapping a hand over my own mouth to keep from shrieking with laughter. Or sexual frustration. Or both.

Chapter 4

Candy

After a quick shower, I wrapped myself in a pink bathrobe, then thumbed through the clothing in Lindyann's closet, looking for something to wear. There was almost nothing: a few pairs of jeans at least two sizes too small for my generous hips, four t-shirts that were so tight they could work as compression bandages for my entire torso, a high school letter jacket, a puffy purple winter coat, what looked like a black, slinky-stretchy cocktail dress, and... "Oh, wow, what is *this*?"

In the very back of the closet, I found what I hoped was a cosplay costume. Only this wasn't any character I recognized. It was a pink furry kitten costume, like an enormous baby onesie, with a very significant flap in the back for... well, I'd leave it at "bathroom access." But the matching buttonable flaps over both nipples and the front opening at the kitty's *kitty area* put that theory to rest.

"Lindyann is a furry?" I giggled. Then the thought of wearing that outfit in front of Nicholas Paxson hit my funny bone just right. I started giggling so hard I thought I might pass out, and raced for my purse. I had to text Rain.

I pulled my phone out, suddenly realizing it had almost no battery life remaining. *Crap.* I called her twice in a row—our emergency signal, since she had a habit of leaving my texts on read for days when she was caught up in trying out new recipes.

"What's happened?" she asked immediately, breathless.

"You will never believe this. I am stuck at the Paxson residence—"

She hissed out a long, whispered, "*Yes...* So you got in? He hired you as his PA?"

"No, a betasitter." I fished around in my purse, looking for my charger cable as I filled her in on the whole debacle. "He thinks I'm a child. Calls me little girl, and not in a sexy, Daddy-dom way." Although, I wasn't a hundred percent sure that was true. The gleam in his eyes as he'd said it... I shook off the fantasy that flickered. Where was my damn charger?

"Listen, this could be exactly what you need," Rain said soothingly. "It's all over the news; this storm will last for days. They're expecting massive snowfall, power outages. You're stuck in the house with him. You can impress him with your professional persona, your skills, your—"

"My omega growl?" I interrupted.

"What?"

"I thought he was taking me to a lover's room, not his sister's. And I fucking *growled.*"

"Oh, shit." The line hummed between us as she considered my words. "Candy, omegas only growl for..."

"Yeah, I watched the video," I muttered. "For compatible alphas."

"No, babe. We only growl when another omega is physically *present* around a super compatible alpha. If you're growling around him without anyone even there, at just the thought of him being near another omega..."

I fought to keep her words from triggering another growl right then. "You can't think he's my—"

The phone battery made the blooping sound of final death, and I sat there, staring at it in my hand. The last two unspoken words burned on my tongue.

True mate.

It couldn't be. I racked my brain for everything I knew about the incredibly rare meetings of two people so compatible, it was as if nature had conspired to create an irresistible pairing. The alphas and omegas who had done interviews for training videos had all said the same thing: that when they first met their true mate, they just *knew.* They had been unable to keep any physical distance between them, and after consummating their love and exchanging mating bites, they shared a psychic emotional link as well as an off-the-charts physical attraction.

And they shared something else: true mated couples almost always had at least a dozen children. They were perfectly genetically compatible, and at least in the stories I'd heard, sometimes even when they used birth control, nature found a fucking way.

Oh shit. Shit shit shit.

I desperately needed to call Rain back, but I didn't have my spare charger. It must be in the car. I peeked out the window. I'd never seen a blizzard this intense; there was no way I was going to be able to get to it now.

I dug in a chest of drawers and found a pair of pajama shorts, then threw them on with the biggest of the t-shirts. My bra was still soaked, so I left it off, grabbing the letter jacket to complete my ridiculous ensemble. It wasn't the worst thing I could have chosen, and I had to get back downstairs. Then, once this storm was over, I had to get out of this house. Maybe even the state.

I wasn't going to entertain the faintest notion of being Nicholas Paxson's true mate. The guy couldn't stand me. But I had to stay. This house was warm, safe, and I had a job. "And a ten-thousand-dollar bonus," I breathed as I wandered back down the hall.

This wing was homier than the others I'd explored, with family photos on the walls. I stopped at one where two beaming parents were surrounded by six children. The mother was heavily pregnant. The dad was an older, silver-haired version of his eldest son, and he wore a smile I couldn't imagine on Nicholas's face.

But there it was. Right in front of me, a teenaged Nicholas himself stood with his hand in his mother's, smiling without any hint of the darkness in his eyes I'd seen today. He must have been around seventeen.

"What happened to change you?" I touched his young face lightly, then shuffled toward the kitchen in the Hello Kitty socks I'd found. Time to start earning my money.

My boss was already in the kitchen, blending something up. His back was to the doorway, but from his seat in his bouncing chair, Benjamin saw me enter and held out his hands, making fists and cooing. I crossed the floor, unbuckled and lifted him out, settling him on one hip. When the blender stopped whirring, I asked casually, "Are you making baby food?"

Nicholas whipped around. "What are you doing? Put him down!"

I lifted an eyebrow. "Why? I'm here to be a sitter. I'm not hurting him. And I would imagine an important man like yourself has work to do. Leave me to take care of the baby."

He scoffed. "You can't imagine that I would leave him in your—what in the hell are you *wearing*?"

I tsked, walking around to the fridge. As the manual had indicated, there were bottles of premade formula inside, along with small glass containers of what I could only assume were bespoke baby food mixtures, probably made with heirloom vegetables grown by twelfth-generation organic farmers. I grabbed one that had *Junegold Peaches* written in perfect calligraphy on a buckwheat paper label, with a small, personalized spoon taped to the top, then closed the fridge with one hip.

When I turned back around, Nicholas was still staring at me, with a look of... revulsion? Yes, that was it. "What. Are. You. Wearing?"

"Your. Sister's. Clothing," I replied, trying to dial back the sass, but failing. Benjamin squealed in my ear, and I bustled over to the highchair, grabbing a burp cloth off the back of it and strapping him in. I thanked heaven for the summer I'd spent in high school working at a theme park; I could buckle squirming kids into roller coasters while anxious parents watched without batting an eye.

I ignored the feeling of being watched as I warmed up the peaches to room temperature using the fancy Bon Appétit Baby sous-vide I'd only ever seen in the fancy kitchen stores my mom loved, then dragged a chair over from the small breakfast table on the other side of the vast kitchen. I sat, opened the baby food, and lifted the spoon to Benjamin's mouth. He shrieked with excitement, managing to immediately spit half of it out. I used the spoon to scrape it back in, before dipping back into the jar for more.

I disregarded the man pacing back and forth on the other side of the kitchen island, more like a lion in a too-small cage than a man. "Is that all she had in her closet?" he growled.

Oh, he wished it was all. I fought back a smile as I shrugged off the bulky letter jacket and draped it over the back of my chair. "The rest didn't fit. I haven't worn those sizes since high school."

"Not that long ago," he grumbled. His voice sounded odd, like he was holding his nose. From the corner of my eye, I saw he was doing just that. I knew the peaches didn't stink, and the baby wasn't dirty.

Yep, he hated my scent. Definitely not my true mate. *Whew.*

"Finish feeding him that, then bring him into my office."

I lifted an eyebrow. "You worried I'm going to abduct him? Feed him more peaches than the manual allows?" I tickled Benjamin's chin with the spoon while he laughed, and said in baby talk, "Curse in front of him like Unky Nik-Nik so he learns new words for Mommy?"

The alpha was silent. I didn't think he was even breathing.

"Tell me about yourself," he said suddenly.

"Why?" I asked, as Benjamin fussed for more peaches. "Don't worry, baby B, I gotchu. Peaches for days in the fridge. We could be snowed in for a month and you won't starve."

"Tell me about yourself," Nicholas repeated. "Somehow, you were hired in one day for a job that normally requires a month of background checks and interviews."

"Wow, really? Betasitting requires top secret clearance?"

"When your parents are billionaires, yes," he said curtly. I nodded, allowing it. "You have no experience at all, from what I can tell."

"How would you know?"

"I did a background check while you showered. I know almost everything there is to know about you. Your unpaid parking ticket near Sycamore University—"

"I was only ten minutes over on the meter!" I interrupted.

"—your unfinished degree at the same university, your

complete lack of job experience in any field, and your only relevant experience—beyond a few high-school gigs as a sitter—as a volunteer for the *Omega League*." He sneered the last words like it was the name of a titty bar.

"Sounds like you already know about me," I replied coolly, ignoring the way he'd dismissed years of taking care of children in homes and at summer camps. He obviously didn't care. "There was no criminal activity, and I never signed anything claiming to have 'relevant' work experience. My résumé is truthful, and it's not my responsibility if your PA didn't vet me as an appropriate replacement." Without turning my head to so much as glance at the alpha, I spooned more peaches into Benjamin's tiny mouth.

"He's new," Nicholas said darkly. The wind whistled so hard around the outside of the house, the walls shook slightly. I rolled my eyes at Benjamin, who giggled.

Yeah, kid. Same.

The man growled slightly. Growled? The *nerve.*

I straightened and stared at him. "Listen, Mr. Paxson. I get that you don't want me here. I'm not a professional betasitter, I'm an omega. But I do have plenty of experience with children. And if I stay here through the end of the year, taking care of this baby, I get paid for my work and a ten-thousand-dollar bonus. I need that money to start my life over. When I'm done, I will leave this house and not darken your door again. I signed an NDA, so I'm legally bound to keep this entire experience secret. I do need the job."

Nicholas crossed his arms over his chest. "You come from a well-off family in the Westclear community, Miss Kane. Your parents have no other children. They have enough money to give you what you ne—"

I stood, fighting the rage tears that threatened. "No one has enough money to give me what I need."

His eyes widened in shock. "What the fuck does *that* mean?"

"You know *why* I have an unfinished degree? Because my university automatically unenrolled me when I presented as an omega, sending a full refund for the final semester along with a letter of congratulations to my parents." I wiped my eyes with the back of one hand. "I had a 4.0 grade average, and a professor who wanted to hire me as a teaching assistant. I had plans for a life where I would be *respected*." I laughed. "And then I woke up one day with my dorm room smelling like what used to be my favorite dessert. And that was the end of having what I needed to be happy: a choice."

His eyes felt heavy on me somehow. Like he was pressing on me with his regard. I folded back into the chair and spooned more peaches into Benjamin's mouth, wiping his face with the cloth.

"What is it you wanted to do?" he asked, just when the silence in the room had stretched me to the breaking point. "Didn't you want a family?"

I scoffed. "Not every omega just wants to be a baby factory. Sure, I wanted kids someday. But after my career was established."

His voice was strangely rough when he finally spoke. "What... What were your professional plans?"

"Nothing amazing. I wasn't hoping to go to med school. I was studying marketing, social media. I had just proposed a senior thesis on how larger companies could use their media footprint as well as donations to make a real impact on fighting poverty around the world."

"Philanthropy. I wouldn't call that 'nothing amazing,'" he muttered. "Your parents didn't fight for you to stay at the university? Omegas can—my sister Lin is an omega. She got her degree." He sounded truly confused.

I let out a soft laugh. "Let me guess: you made sure she had the very highest-grade pheromone blockers so she could attend classes? They let her take her exams privately, so the hormones she released during stressful times didn't affect anyone else? They probably excused her absences during her heats."

He made an odd sound at that. I kept feeding the baby, who was now fingerpainting in dribbles of peach on his tray and babbling soft nonsense words. A few sounded like mama and dada, but I had the feeling he was trying to say peach, too.

"My parents are well off, but not like this. And they were so *proud* of me. It's supposed to be a status thing, you know? An omega born into their family tree for the first time ever? They were over the moon. Started alpha shopping that very evening, while I cried."

"Alpha shopping?"

I nodded at the horror in his tone. "You think unclaimed omegas get to stay that way? When we're not permitted to work most jobs, not allowed to get a degree? I was a miracle baby, a late-in-life surprise. My parents say they need to see me 'taken care of' before they die, and they think finding an alpha is the best way to do that. As I recall, they waited an entire day to sign me up for Knotmate.com."

"For *what* the fuck?" he barked.

I froze as his alpha bark pinned me in place. I'd never heard a bark at such close range, and for a moment, I was afraid I might wet myself. Palpable waves of rage flooded the kitchen. I held my breath, praying it would stop soon.

And then the anger was washed out of the kitchen in a split second, as Benjamin lifted his peach-covered face and said distinctly, "Fuck."

Chapter 5

Pax

The young woman in my kitchen was going to be the death of me. My inner voice corrected me: *No, that'll be your sister, after she learns you taught her one-year-old to say* fuck.

She hadn't answered my question, and I'd fled the room in embarrassment. Not just at cursing, but at the way I'd lost control of my alpha impulses. I hadn't barked in the presence of an omega since... Well, at least for a few years. For most of my adult life, omegas had hounded me, setting up all sorts of situations to try and force me to claim one of them. They'd engineered a ridiculous number of stunts to get close enough to "prove" they were my true mate. I'd barked at one particularly persistent one who'd tried to corner me in a men's toilet at the opera.

Honestly, if I hadn't realized this bundle of strawberries and cream was my true mate, I'd have thought she was another alpha-chaser. Well, and if I hadn't already had my investigator pull everything from her pediatric dental records to her high school yearbook.

Shit, almost all her memories would be from high school, or before. I was such a fucking deviant, staring at her, sniffing at her, like this. Until today, I'd thought never meeting my true mate was an ugly trick fate had played. Now I knew she'd had a worse trick up her sleeve: sending me one I couldn't claim. Not if I considered myself a decent man, and a decent alpha.

No. It wasn't fate who'd done this. It was Theodore Sands. I stormed to my home office, grabbed my phone, and called my old PA. Damn him for retiring. Seventy wasn't that old to still be working, was it?

Edward answered promptly, though I could hear his family singing Christmas carols in the background. "Yes, Mr. Paxson? Is everything all right?"

"No. You have to come back to work. I'm going to fire my new PA, and no one else can do this job."

"No one else wants to put up with you, huh?" He laughed. "Give him a while. He'll figure it out. Do you still have electricity?"

"Yes, why?"

"The grid is down in a large part of the city, and they've closed the roads. I know you've got the baby there. You have enough food, I hope? I'm fairly sure your household staff won't be able to make it in until after Christmas."

Fuck. I hadn't even considered that. Alone with that tempting omega until the snow melted. "I'm not helpless, Ed. I raised nine siblings. I can cook a few meals."

The music cut off; Edward had gone to a different room. "What's up, Pax? Something's wrong."

I sighed. "I'm sorry. I'll let you get back to your family." After he'd thanked me for the gifts I'd sent his grandkids, I hung up and made another call. "Theodore, I need information. What is a thing called Knotmate.com?"

"The matchmaking service?" His voice broke like a

teenager. "Sir, if you want me to make you a profile, I am happy to do so, but I'd much rather try to set up a few dates with select indivi—"

"No, I don't want to fucking date. Tell me about the service." I rubbed my forehead as he went on to gush about the matchmaking service for the elite that specialized in finding "close enough" matches for wealthy alphas who'd given up on finding their true mate.

The mother of all headaches was coming on. Probably due to lack of blood flow to my brain; I'd had a hard-on since I'd first smelled that luscious omega in my front hall.

"Are you sure you don't want me to create an anonymous profile?" Theodore asked. "You could go on a few dates. Who knows, your true mate could be right around the corner!"

"You have no idea," I grunted and hung up. I made a mental note to actually fire my PA once this storm was over. He seemed far too keen on discussing my mate status.

I sat there, wondering what the hell to do. I wanted a whiskey, but I knew better. If I couldn't control my own bark stone-cold sober, after a glass or three of Balvenie, I'd probably last five minutes before I'd have my knot stretching her tight cunt and my teeth in her neck.

My cock gave a jerk in my pants, and I glared down at it. She wouldn't want an old, dried-up bachelor, even if she did feel the true mate bond, which she'd shown no signs of noticing. That made me a little more bitter than I liked to admit.

Was it just me? She had come into her status later than most. Maybe she would have a delayed reaction to my presence, my pheromones. If I stayed away from her, she could go on her merry way as soon as the roads cleared. I'd give her the damn bonus. Fuck, I'd find her a job in an international branch of Paxson Pharma. She deserved that, deserved happiness, and a chance at the life she'd chosen before.

Not a tired old alpha who felt like the worst sort of degenerate every time those cherry-pink nipples poked through my little sister's t-shirt.

I could fix the clothing issue. I'd get her a shirt to layer over the inappropriate tee. And some sweats. And a sweater vest. That was it. I would cover her so completely in clothing that I wouldn't be able to see her curvy, irresistible, biteable body. That's what I would do.

The baby monitor on my desk began playing a song that was vaguely familiar, about wanting to build a snowman, if completely out of tune. Then the woman's voice stopped singing, and said, "Benjamin, you are such a good boy. I'm going to teach you to say some nice words, so when your mommy comes home, she doesn't cut-cut your Unky Nik-Nik's wiener off. Cut cut cut!"

Benjamin repeated, "Cut cut cut!"

For the first time all day, my cock went the slightest bit soft. "I'll take it as a win," I muttered and stood, heading to my bedroom to find clothing that would work to make that tasty omega into a snowman.

A half hour later, I knew exactly where to find Candace and Benjamin from the racket. I just wasn't certain why they were still in that room, and not the nursery.

She was on the kitchen floor with him, her back to me, both of them beating on the copper bottoms of Chef Adaline's French stockpots. She'd pulled her dark hair up into a messy knot on top of her head. Her skin was pink and flushed with exertion and laughter as she yelled out, "Drum solo!"

Benjamin had obviously figured out this game because he

screamed, "Dum!" and whacked the pot over and over with one hand.

I stared as she scooted across the marble floor to sit behind him, wrapping her arms around him and letting him hold a spoon in each hand. "If you can figure out how to use both hands to play the drums, I can get you a gig in a band downtown. My friends' drummer moved away. Honestly, you have more talent in your little finger than Rory did in both arms." With her arms over his, she beat out a *rat-a-tat* that had Benjamin screaming for more.

"He won't have the motor skills to play with both hands for at least another two years, possibly more," I said when they stopped for a break. She twisted her head around, enough to acknowledge my presence, but didn't look at me. Her sweet scent went slightly bitter, like burned crème brûlée. It bothered me more than it should. "Are you afraid of me?" I asked quietly.

Her shoulders rounded, like she was trying to curl into a ball. "Mr. Paxson, please don't take this the wrong—"

"Pax," I interrupted. "Or Nick. My siblings call me Nicky. My friends call me Pax." I wanted her to call me that. Yell it, as she came apart under my hands, my tongue.

"Mr. Paxson," she repeated, a little more starch in her tone. It pleased me to hear. "I think if you're going to bark again, you should stay in your office. Benjamin's bedtime is in an hour. I'll stay in your sister's room, and you don't even need to see me."

"Good," I said, hating how she flinched. "I put clothing for you in her room, on the bed."

"I can just wear th—"

"No." I cut her off again, and she shivered slightly. *Damnit.* When had I become the kind of alpha who terrified young omegas?

About three hours ago, apparently.

43

I softened my tone. "I checked the weather reports. We're stuck here for at least two days, maybe through Christmas, or longer if the temperatures stay low and the trucks can't get to us." Though I would buy a fleet of snowplows if I had to, to escape this intoxicating woman before I did something more shameful, and more permanent, than barking at her. "You'll need more clothing. And I want you to know..." I cleared my throat. "I am deeply sorry for barking earlier. That's not who I am. My mother would have been ashamed. I am ashamed. Even if you won't be staying for all the days you agreed to, I will pay you the contracted amount and provide the bonus as well. Only, you must accept my apology."

"You can't buy an apology," she said softly. My heart dropped, but she finished, "They're free if you ask sincerely. I forgive you, Mr. Paxson."

"Thank you," I murmured, and backed out of the room. It was the hardest thing I had done in years, and it was only stepping away. But removing myself from her presence was the only way to keep myself from losing control of my inner nature completely.

From answering the drumbeat insistence that thrummed in my mind: *Mate. Claim. Mine.*

I managed it for a day. I carried food into my office, placed rolled-up bath towels along the bottom of the closed doors to keep her scent from drifting in, and only came out to piss or grab more food. Once, I heard her humming in the kitchen, and I crept back into my office like I was the one who didn't belong here. I needed the distraction of work, but all the offices were closed in this part of the country, and everyone else was off on fucking vacations. So instead, I cyber-stalked the precocious omega upstairs.

She really had been an exemplary student in high school and college. That she had gotten kicked out made me angry enough to send a letter to the Vice-Provost of Finance, an old friend of my father's, with her case as the reason I would be withdrawing all my pledged donations for the next ten years and calling into question the university's ethics as well.

That made me feel slightly less feral.

Even better was when I called the older brother of the founder of Knotmate.com. He and I had gone sailing around the Maldives one summer, and for the price of my boat—the one he'd lusted after almost embarrassingly—he agreed to find a way to disable any requests for Candace's "knot mates."

Fucking ridiculous. Knotting an omega didn't mean you were a mate. A mate bond like the one my parents had shared was sacred, and special, and...

I pressed my face into the sofa cushion and screamed as loud as I could. Then I jerked off into another dish towel—the seventh time that day—and threw it into my office trash can.

Next, I looked into the paper-thin online presence of the Blue Skies "agency" where Theodore had apparently found Candace. I left the website alone—it was highly unlikely anyone else would hire them, since it was obvious they were three or four girls in a metaphorical trench coat, pretending to be a business—but I called Theodore and fired him, mere days before Christmas.

That was shitty timing, even for me. I immediately called him back and apologized, giving him a raise. He mumbled a snarky, "God bless us every one," Scrooge reference before hanging up. I made a note in my calendar to fire him the day after Christmas instead.

After twenty-eight hours of no sleep—because I knew

fucking better than to walk that close to her door, as Lin would never forgive me for the acts I was fantasizing about committing on top of her hideously ugly homemade quilt—I broke. I called the only person who I thought might give me good advice.

"Storm here," he answered on the first ring. "What the fuck do you want, Pax?"

"I want you to drive out in this storm, bring whatever weapon you can lay hands on, and put me down like a rabid skunk."

He paused for a moment, then burst into laughter. "If driving out in this shit wasn't certain to kill me first, I'd help. I've wanted to get you back ever since the Everson buyout." I laughed along with him. "All I have is a shovel anyway. And paintball guns. What's up, Pax?"

I outlined the situation for him, and he cursed soundly when I was done, then went quiet. Besides my parents, Lin, and Victor, Storm was the only person I knew who had a true mate. He'd met her five years before, when he was twenty-nine. He was younger than me, but that didn't matter between friends like us, who had so much in common.

But some age gaps were insurmountable. He'd scented her first, then seen her, at a park on vacation, buying ice cream cones from a vendor, and accompanied by a large family. He hadn't approached her, but he'd asked the vendor her age. She'd looked to be younger than eighteen, though most omegas didn't perfume until then. The vendor had told Storm they'd been celebrating her fourteenth birthday. He'd asked around, and learned it was true. She was the oldest daughter of a large, happy family, according to their hotel concierge.

Storm had walked away right then, moved to the East Coast, and never seen her since. He was honorable, but the fight not to go to her had almost broken that honor.

He'd turned to a lot of methods to tame his inner, raging alpha nature. To stop himself from turning into some sort of crazed pedophile. Meditation and yoga, booze, extreme sports, and finally, medication. And not just any medication: he was one of a very few who knew Paxson Pharma had started human trials for a new hormone suppressant for alphas.

"How are the drugs working?" I asked. I should know; Storm had become one of my best friends after he'd moved a few miles down the street. "Think they'd slip me into the study?" I laughed, but he didn't join me.

"They're not good," he said quietly. "I'm going to have to try something else. The doctors think it's causing heart damage."

"Fuck." My own heart panged. "How old would your mate be now? Nineteen, right?" Still not old enough; I knew that.

"I can't talk about it." His voice was choked, and he stopped to clear his throat before continuing. "But listen... if she had been twenty-four when I met her? I wouldn't have walked away. Maybe you should try. Ask her. Isn't she going nuts, pursuing you? Mature omegas, man. They're a force of nature." We both sighed; we'd been chased by enough of them to know.

"She was a late bloomer," I told him. "I don't think she feels it like I do."

"Well then, the answer to what you should do seems pretty clear." The line buzzed, and he sighed again before adding, "Find out."

Chapter 6

Candy

In the Omega League trainings, they'd tried to tell us omegas were natural-born mothers. Even though I'd always wanted kids eventually, I'd thought that theory was a sack of shit—just more of the stuff they were trying to sell us to make it seem like we weren't being forced away from real lives and jobs. That mothering was what we were best suited for, though we weren't supposed to be drawn to other women's children.

But I was killing this betasitting gig. I'd missed being around kids more than I'd realized.

"I wonder why they don't let omegas work as nannies? I think we're better. We can calm you little guys down, and we already like soft blankets and sweet foods..." Benny and I were finger painting with some fancy bath paints on the side of his tub. I hadn't seen Pax for an entire day and a half—Mr. Paxson, I reminded myself firmly—but I'd sensed him, and even heard his office door open a few times. He was obviously avoiding me, which was fine. I could live my whole life without being barked at again, thank you very much.

I leaned over the tub, using the purple paint to draw a big dick on the far side of the tub. "That's your Unky Nik-Nik," I murmured. "A big old meanie dick-dick."

"If I get in trouble for teaching him bad words, I think you should, too," a deep, gravelly voice said right behind me.

I closed my eyes in humiliation. "Sorry, Mr. Paxson."

"I told you not to call me that." He sat on the toilet, and even though I'd glanced at him and looked away, I could feel his eyes boring into me. "That's two, angel."

"Two what?" He growled at me slightly. "Two what, sir?" I amended.

"You'll find out if you get to three."

I clenched my thighs together in the thin sleep shorts I was still wearing, hoping the damp patch wasn't obvious. Or maybe hoping it was. The man was probably used to omegas practically floating away from slick spills every time he walked past. I snorted at the mental image and crooned a few lines of "Row Row Row Your Boat."

"You're a terrible singer," he remarked. "You sound like a cat being bathed."

When I shrieked in protest, Benjamin splashed me, babbling the unmistakable word "fuck" over and over. I slanted a glance at the hulking alpha, who... Oh, sweet, muscled temptations, he'd rolled the sleeves of his white dress shirt up his forearms and was leaning toward me, just... *flexing* them at me.

"Cover yourself," I hissed.

He scowled. "What do you mean?" He shifted forward, flexing those forearms again.

"That's indecent," I muttered, standing to face him. "You come in here, half naked..." I trailed off. His jaw had dropped open, and he was staring at my tits again. "Honestly, didn't anyone ever teach you that eyes are up *here*?"

He blushed, snapping his gaze to my face. "Why aren't you

wearing my clothes?" he snarled. I put my hands on my hips, ignoring Benny's splashing around for a moment as I realized... Yup. I was once again wearing a wet shirt and no bra.

"Well, fancy seeing you two," I muttered to my nipples.

"Did you just talk to your breasts?" He ran a hand over his face.

"Listen, if you had a pair this unruly, you'd need to keep them in line as well." Mischief possessing me, I lifted them up, one in each hand, and said firmly, "If you two don't settle down, I will punish you in the worst possible way." Pax let out a strange whimpering sound, and I finished, "I will force you into a bra after ten p.m." I looked back at my employer. "Now, if you don't mind, it's time for me to put the baby to bed, and then toddle off to my own room." Where I would most likely masturbate five times before I could fall asleep, like I had the nights before.

I would've thought I was getting close to a heat cycle with how oversexed I'd been feeling, but I'd just had one two months ago, so wasn't due for ten more months, thank goodness. But my skin also felt itchy and tingly, like I was allergic to something. Maybe the laundry detergent? I hoped I wasn't getting sick. I needed the money, but I wouldn't risk Benjamin's health to get it.

I pulled him out of the tub and wrapped him in a towel, pretending Pax wasn't in the room. After putting a fresh diaper on the baby, I gave him the bottle from the handy bedside bottle warmer and settled him on my lap to read *Goodnight Moon* six times in a row, until he was finally drowsy enough to go to bed. Then I turned the monitor on, and tiptoed out.

Pax had left a moment before, and was waiting in the hallway.

"What?" I asked, forcing myself to look into his face. The storm clouds on his brow were scary. "...sir?"

A slow, almost sinister smile formed. "Damn, I thought we'd get to three." He reached out with one hand to gently touch the base of my throat, where my pulse was thudding. "Come on, princess. Let's get some dinner."

I followed him downstairs, wondering when my neck had become a primary erogenous zone—honestly, it had felt almost as good as being touched between my thighs—and was shocked when we reached the kitchen. The island had two of the plush padded bar stools pulled up, and there was what looked like a steak pie and a green salad next to the two place settings, along with a peach cobbler, still bubbling on the side of the stove.

"How? When did you make this?" I was stunned. I'd only been upstairs for an hour and a half.

"My chef called earlier this morning. She's beside herself that she wasn't able to come to prepare the Christmas meals. But she had me pull these out of the freezer to thaw this morning, and I popped it into the oven when you went upstairs. You're following that ridiculous schedule very faithfully. I'm impressed."

My skin prickled again. So he had been paying as much attention to my whereabouts as I had his. "Well, thank you," I told him, sitting down on the stool he pulled out for me. "Better than the energy bar dinner I'd planned."

"You're welcome, princess," he said, brushing past me.

He kept that up for the whole meal, touching me lightly, brushing a hand across mine as he reached for the salad, asking me to pass him the bottle of red wine and then moving his fingers over mine when I did.

All the casual touches were driving me crazy.

But worse were the questions. He asked me everything from what my childhood pets had been, to what I liked to eat for breakfast, to my favorite poets. I tried not to be offended when he acted shocked that I could quote Hafiz, Rumi, Dickinson, and Wendell Berry. "I'll pull some of my books for you to read," he promised, his eyes boring into me like I was some great mystery.

I knew what I was. A young, unaccomplished omega who was probably going to end up back at her parents' house in a week, and married to a man with a booger nose within a year. The thought made me drink faster.

By the time we got to the questions about old boyfriends, I had worked my way through half the bottle of wine, and I would have told him my mother's maiden name, my social security number, and my social media passwords without blinking.

"So, did you have any serious boyfriends?" he asked too casually, rolling his wine glass by the stem in one hand.

"Are you trying to find out if I'm a"—I hiccupped—"a virgin, Mr. Paxson, sir?" I ran my finger over the rim of my own wine glass. "Because the answer is no. I had plenty of boy—hic! —boyfriends. Well, three is plenty, right?"

"More than enough," he gritted out.

I noticed a spill of wine on the counter and then saw him throw the two pieces of his glass in the trash. When had that broken?

"No alpha boyfriends, though," I said, leaning my head on my hand with a sigh. "I mean, not that I had the chance. We all thought I was a beta until just a few years—hic!—ago. And then, when I did start my heats, my parents' stupid doctor friends all said not to let me spend them with alphas, in case I got bitten and ended up with 'the wrong sort.'" I made air quotes that somehow tipped the wine bottle over. But Pax caught it. I patted his forearm, praising him. "You're so fast. Super fast. I bet you're the fastest alpha in the state."

For some reason, he laughed. "I promise I can go slow."

"Well, if I go back home, my parents will probably guilt me into marrying Andreas, who *is* an alpha."

"Omegas get to *choose* their mates," he said, his tone chilling. "They can't force you."

"But what if my choice was not to end up with any alpha?" I muttered. "Why did I have to lose everything? All I wanted was a choice."

"So you'd settle for this alpha... Andreas?"

"Probably." I sighed. "Andreas Vanderwall III. Can you imagine me named Candy Vanderwall III? He's not an alpha like you, though."

"How is he not like me?" he growled, and the hair on my arms stood up. "Is he young?"

"Ugh, he is so young. Same age as me. I've known him since we were four." I shivered. "Creepy guy. Not touchy-creepy, but looky-creepy. My parents, though, are easily impressed by his alpha bloodline. His great-great-something grandfather was the Alpha Captain on the Mayflower." I rolled my eyes.

"His bloodline?" For some reason, Pax had his phone out in his hand and was typing in something.

"Oh my god, are you looking him up?"

He shoved his phone back into his pocket. "Of course not." But his lips were tight.

"What about you? Any girlfriends?" I probed subtly, letting my eyes run up and down his muscular frame. He still had a suit on, and I wondered what he would look like in jeans. Or a swimsuit. Or maybe just socks.

"My feet *are* one of my best features," he muttered for some reason as he stood, rinsed out my wine glass, and refilled it with water. "Shame to cover them up." He handed me the glass. I sneered at it, until he growled, "Drink it down, princess. Every drop."

"I don't like water," I complained. "I liked the wine." Suddenly, a warm, firm hand was on the back of my neck, and my face was tilted up. His other hand wrapped around the wineglass and lifted it to my lips.

"Be a good girl and drink it all." Our eyes met, and the stern command in his voice had my core starting a spiral that had only ever happened when I was ten minutes into a self-care session.

"Oh fuck," I managed to say before I was swallowing slowly, his thumb moving over my throat.

"Every drop, beautiful. That's right, such a good girl."

I whimpered when the glass was done, and felt my jaw drop open slightly when he brushed his thumb over the corner of my mouth, catching one stray droplet, and then feeding it into my mouth. I couldn't blink, couldn't look away. What was he doing?

His thumb dipped in between my lips, and he pressed down on my tongue, his eyes still blazing. "Suck, Omega," he commanded, and I did, feeling the hot press of his thumb go a little deeper. Like he was testing me. Preparing me to take something bigger.

Suddenly, he let out a soft purr, the vibrations traveling all the way from where he touched my neck down to my clit, and I clenched so hard I thought I might fall off my stool.

And then he backed away. "Time for bed, princess."

Yes. I nodded. That was exactly what I wanted.

He took my hand, leading me upstairs. At some point on the staircase, I slipped, and he scooped me up, carrying me.

"I like this," I slurred. "I'm not little like the other omegas. Too tall, you know. Big bones." He muttered something about his own big bone, and I snorted. "You make me feel small."

"You are small, princess. Small and young and fucking forbidden."

I had no idea what he meant by that, but when he poured

me into the pink and purple bed, then quietly slid the door shut, leaving me alone, I got the idea.

The next day, Benny cooing the word, "Fuck," repeatedly woke me up.

"Charming," I told him as I walked into the nursery.

All day, I kept waiting for Pax to appear. And all day, he stayed in his office. Once, during Benny's nap, I stood outside his office door. There was no sound at all, but when I pressed my ear to the door, I heard an unmistakable groan. Was he watching porn? I leaned closer, holding my breath, and heard him moan my name and the words, "Good girl."

That sent me to my own room to abuse myself. I hadn't masturbated this much since my last heat. For some reason, that thought made me go a little nuts. The room I was in seemed suddenly too bright, the quiet music too loud. The blankets were all wrong, too. The only things that were right were the shirts and sweatpants Pax had brought for me to wear. The ones I leaked slick through so fast when I did try to wear them, I kept having to take them off immediately. I carried them to the closet, foggily thinking that maybe it was time to put them away.

When Benjamin began fussing, I was still in the closet arranging things. I ran out as soon as he cried, though, and went to get his afternoon snack—heirloom green bean purée—and some more educational toys. If my phone had been charged, I would definitely have turned on a non-educational show so I could rest. But the sitter manual had specified that screen time should be minimal, and I wasn't about to interrupt Pax to ask where a television was, or if I could use a computer.

So playtime it was. When Benny finally went to bed for the night, I went to my room as well. I didn't even eat dinner. For some reason, I wasn't hungry or thirsty. I was just prickly. Annoyed. Why had Pax spent the evening before asking me about myself? Being charming and sticking his thumb in my mouth and telling me to suck? He'd seemed like he cared about me. Like he wanted to be with me. No—like he *needed* to be with me. He hadn't been able to look away.

Whatever. He was an asshole alpha, and I was done masturbating over him.

I went back to the closet to finish putting all the things into the right places, then pulling them out and doing it again. And again.

Chapter 7

Pax

After I'd tucked Candy into my sister's bed and watched her sleep for over two hours, like some pervert who needed to be in jail, I'd finally gone back to my office and managed to drink enough to fall into unconsciousness.

My inner voice was screaming at me to go back into that room, wake her up with my knot locked deep in her pussy, and show her exactly what an alpha my age could do with his omega mate. But every time I thought that, I forced myself to repeat her age out loud a hundred times, and think of my own little sisters.

Would I want them with a crusty, overworked alpha like me? Fuck no.

And her words kept echoing in my memory. *"But what if my choice was not to end up with any alpha? Why did I have to lose everything?"*

All she'd wanted was a choice. And I could fucking give her that.

So, I spent my energy setting up a paid internship that was

tailored to the classes she had completed at Sycamore University, took a dozen apologetic phone calls from every level of leadership at the university up to and including the president—who may have been crying as he begged me to reinstate the funding for the football team in particular.

Then I started looking into high-security apartments near campus. She was not going to have to move back in with her parents and be forced to marry some sniveling alpha kid who had a video game addiction, a history of drunk driving, and an unfortunate medical history that included allergies, an unspecified bladder control issue, and an STD that had been cleared up with antibiotics the year prior.

I knew I had lost my mind. I was calling in favors that I'd accrued for a decade, stalking everyone who had ever crossed paths with this girl I needed to leave alone. It felt like the least I could do.

My sister had called to check on Benjamin, and I realized I hadn't even seen my nephew that day. I was a coward, hiding in my office. I made myself a promise to spend the whole day with him tomorrow, which was... I checked my calendar. It was Christmas Eve tomorrow? *Fuck.* I didn't have anything for dinner ready or a gift for Candy. Though I could fix that last one.

I had just offered an anonymous entrepreneurship grant to the Blue Skies agency when I heard something crashing upstairs. In my wing.

In her fucking room.

I raced up the stairs, down the hall, and threw open the door. "What happened?" The room was dark, and all I could hear was a whimpering sound over by the... closet? "Candy? Are you all right?"

I flicked on the light, but she shrieked, "Too bright!" so I immediately turned it off. Pausing for a moment, I sucked in a breath. I had never smelled any omega perfume this rich, this thick. I crossed to the opposite wall and turned on a small floor lamp instead.

"Princess, are you okay?"

"N-no," she sobbed, and I raced to the closet door. Had she hurt herself? The light was just strong enough to see that one of the clothing rods had fallen on top of her.

"Let me help," I murmured, stepping into the closet.

She hissed, the sound of a cornered cat. I waited, letting my eyes adjust. The closet floor was lined with pillows, and... my clothing. It wasn't thrown in either. It was arranged, with a lip of pillows around the perimeter of the rough circle, and the shirts and sweats carefully pleated over the edges.

My heart went cold. My cock went hard. And my knot swelled up.

My little omega had built a fucking nest.

How had this happened? She hadn't smelled like she was in heat. She'd smelled good, but not... *Oh shit*. One instance of my sister's oversharing echoed in my head.

"I couldn't help it, Nicky. He loaned me his coat, and then he dropped me off—we were going to wait! But in four hours, I was turning my apartment into Fort Blanketlandia, and in so much pain, I had to call him."

She'd reminded me there were two kinds of heats: the normal cyclical one, which came once a year. And the mating heat, which only happened if an omega met her true mate, and they were close enough for her to feel he'd accepted her. Or would accept her.

I'd done this. I'd given her my clothing. I'd filled the whole house with my pheromones. I'd stuck my damned *thumb* in her mouth.

"Alpha," she whimpered. Not Mr. Paxson, Pax, or Nicholas. Not even sir.

Alpha.

I steeled myself. I knew I had to turn around, put distance between us. I could go jump in the fifteen-foot snow drifts at the fence line to cool off. But I couldn't leave her buried under all Lin's clothing. She could be hurt under there, beaned in the head by the metal rod, for fuck's sake. I had to see her, make sure she was all right. Then I would go.

"Can I help you, Omega?" I asked quietly. "Can I come into your nest and help?"

Chapter 8

Candy

"Can I come into your nest and help?"

I almost sobbed in relief when I heard Pax's gentle words. Okay, I actually did sob. "Yes, please," I finally managed to say, clawing at the clothing that had fallen on top of me. I was fairly certain the kitten costume had landed directly on my head, and I was as equally horrified at that as I was at the knowledge that Nicholas Paxson had seen my pathetic first attempt at nest-building using his clothing.

But warring with horror for my dominant emotion was joy. He had just offered to come into my nest and help me, which I'd thought was the last thing Mr. "Avoid The Sitter At All Costs" would say. I felt the terrible cat costume being lifted away, and covered my face with my hands. Not because the light was harsh, but because I had been crying off and on for an entire day, and I knew my face had swelled up like a giant strawberry.

Then I felt hands on my hair, fingers threading through the tangled mess. "I need to see your eyes, love. I need to check for a concussion."

I had to look up then. *Love?* "It... It didn't hit my head."

"You screamed like you were hurt," he growled. "Your face. Something's wrong with it." I tried to cover it again, but he lifted me up, so the light from the other room fell on it. "You've been..."

"Crying, okay?" I burst out. "I've been crying, and now I need you to go away so I can cry some more."

"Why?" His hands kept running through my hair, his clever fingers undoing the tangles that had formed. I closed my eyes and let myself lean into him. I knew he might push me away, but maybe he would hold me up for a moment. And if a moment was all I could get with him, I would take it.

I lifted my face to his, and as fast as I could, I laid a quick, dry kiss on his lips.

He held still, then gave a groan and wrapped his arms around my waist, lifting me off the floor. He ravaged my mouth, his tongue forcing its way in between my lips, his hands holding me so tight it might leave bruises on my ass. I hoped it did. I wanted him to mark me everywhere.

His cock was rock hard, almost painfully so, as he pressed it into my groin. I could feel the thickening of the knot that had formed at the base, and I wanted nothing more than to feel that. Finally, to feel what it would be like to be stretched that wide, to be overcome with the pain and pleasure of it, to have my body owned by my alpha.

Claimed as *his.*

I knew he would. He'd asked permission to enter my nest, hadn't he? Asked to help me. No alpha could resist an omega in need. No honorable one would leave an omega wanting.

"Fuck me, Alpha," I mumbled when he began kissing down my neck, his teeth scraping against my neck. "Bite me."

He froze, his breath hissing in and out like he'd been running up a mountain. "I can't... I won't take that from you."

What the hell did that mean?

Before I could form words to ask, my gut cramped up as a rush of fluid spilled from between my legs onto the pillows and clothing beneath me. He groaned again, and lowered me slowly until I was standing.

"Why have you been crying, princess?" He tucked my hair behind my ears, cupping my cheeks. I felt a soft, strong purring sound start up in his chest, and I pressed my hips against him, rubbing on that hard cock again. He wasn't kissing me now, but this was almost as good.

"You don't want me," I said before I could stop myself. "You know, that's the only thing about being an omega I thought might be good. That someday I would meet an alpha I would want. And he would want me back. And you gave me all these clothes, and then you just... left."

I smelled his clean, pure scent change, his body stiffening. Was he angry?

"I'm so sorry, love. I'm so sorry. I should never have given you those clothes. I don't know what I was thinking. I've been trying to stay away—"

I threw myself away from him, across the closet, burying my face in shame. "Go away. Oh, god, go *away*. It *hurts*." The ache in my core, the pain from the heat, was nothing compared to the agony inflicted by his words. I wanted to claw my own eyes out so I wouldn't keep wanting to stare at him. Wanted to tear my heart out, it hurt so much.

"Princess, I can't leave you."

"Please go. You already hurt me enough."

"How?" His question hung in the air.

He needed me to spell it out? I lifted my face, speaking to the back wall of this closet. "You can see what I've done. I built a nest. I invited you in. If you're not going to help me, if you just came to torture me with what I can't have, leave me alone."

"I didn't mean—" he began, but I screamed, "*Go!*"

I cried so hard, I thought I would run out of tears even before I felt him turn away. I sensed the lessening of his almost-oppressive pheromones as the outer door opened and closed with a soft click.

I wept and suffered, wondering if it was possible to die from a combination of humiliation, heartache, and sexual frustration. My mind was fuzzy, though not as much as a normal heat. So I knew what I'd been asking, when I'd begged him to bite me, claim me.

But I'd been almost certain. No, I *was* certain. He was my true mate. Omegas only ever had these weird mini-heats when they met their one perfect match. And I was so lacking, so pathetic... I held my breath, hoping I would pass out and not have to feel any more.

A gravelly voice broke the silence of the sad nest. "I brought you some things, Omega."

He'd come back? I smelled the sharp tang of fruit and the mellow softness of cheese, and hunched into a ball. Why had he returned? To gloat, taunt me? Tell me how young and insufficient I was?

Before I could think of a reason, I felt his arms circling me, warmth enfolding me as he pulled me onto his lap, my back to his broad, warm chest. "You need to eat, Omega." His purr rumbled up from his diaphragm, setting everything inside me thrumming with anticipation. I kept my eyes shut. He needed to stop calling me Omega. The way he said it made it sound like a title instead of only a descriptor. Like I was *his* omega.

"Just leave it and go," I mumbled. "I'll eat later."

"You'll eat now, Candy. And from my hand." My eyes snapped open, and my jaw dropped. For a moment, that thumb was in my mouth again, pulling my lower jaw even wider. "Look at that sweet mouth, open for me. What a good girl," he purred louder in my ear, then fed a bite of sharp cheddar cheese between my lips. "Now swallow."

He repeated the motions, until the plate of cheese and soft bread and the cup of pineapple juice was gone. Then he reached around me with both arms and began to slowly unbutton the front of the dress shirt I'd scavenged from his pile.

"You are the most beautiful woman I've ever seen," he said, his voice so low and monotone it was almost a hum. His purring never stopped, and I pressed my hands on the tops of his thighs to feel more of it. "When you walked into my house, I wanted to throw you down on the floor and knot you, claim you, right then. Take this body and worship it the way perfection like this deserves. With my hands, and my lips."

He ran his nose up the side of my throat as he undid the final button, opening the shirt to expose my breasts. He hummed, scraping his short beard along the length of my neck, as he encircled both breasts with his massive hands, his fingers rolling the tight pink nubs around gently at first, then harder. Dizzy with the sensations, I gasped as he spent the next few moments nibbling at me and kissing, while exploring the line between not enough and too much pressure on my nipples.

He pinched one of them harder as he reached down with the other hand to part my dark, trimmed curls, and ran a thick finger through my wet lips. "Dripping for your alpha like the good girl I know you can be. Spread your legs, princess, wide as you can." He tilted his hips forward so I could feel the length of his cock pressing against my back, and I rubbed against it like a cat while I obeyed. "Look at that," he purred. "Open your eyes."

I did, and saw what he meant. The back of the closet had a gilt-framed, floor-to-ceiling mirror, and the scene reflected in it was obscene and beautiful at the same time.

"Watch yourself, princess. Watch how this pretty pussy gives me what I need." He ran the backs of his nails over my inner thighs, his other hand still torturing my nipple, then slowly circled closer and closer to my swollen, glistening clit. I was dripping slick all over the clothing beneath us, and he gathered some of my fluid up and began to circle my clit faster, every so often dipping into my channel for more.

"God, I have to taste that." He brought his hand up to his mouth, sucking his fingers. "Fucking delicious. Gonna drink every drop you give me, Omega." I began to shiver, my orgasm approaching already. His fingers returned to the center of my pleasure, winding circles at just the right tempo, just the right pressure. "Look in my eyes, princess, when you come. Look at me, and see who's giving you your orgasm. The first of many."

Meeting his gaze in the mirror was terrifying, the way this exposed not just my physical needs, but my emotions. Still, I did as he commanded. I stared into his glowing, nearly jet-black eyes as I fell over the cliff, shouting, "Pax!"

He gentled me down from the spirals of pleasure for no more than a minute, then moved his thick fingers to my wet slit and plunged inside, curving them to hit that perfect spot that was still connected to my throbbing clit by a thick cord of pleasure.

"Too much," I cried out, twisting away from his probing hand, but he moved his grip from my breast to my throat, and turned my face to the mirror again.

"Do you really want this to stop now, Omega? Are you sure you want all this pleasure to come... to... a halt..." He slowed his thrusts as he spoke, and I whimpered.

"No. Please don't stop," I managed to squeak out.

He kissed my temple, murmuring, "Such a good girl, you've earned a reward." He picked up his pace and fucked me with three fingers, stretching me wide and making my pussy clench helplessly in another near-painful orgasm as he promised dark, depraved deeds, whispering in my ear how many times he was going to fuck me, and where. "Everywhere is mine tonight, sweet girl. I'm going to lay you down now, and then I'll work my fat cock into that sweet, tight cunt." He pressed my hands over my head to hold onto a velvet pillow. "Don't let go," he warned, then stood to strip his own clothing away.

My mouth went dry at the muscles on his torso, the Adonis belt that led down to a proud, angry cock that was easily twice as thick as any beta's I'd ever encountered. Much thicker than the toy I'd bought online for my heats. The knot at the base was terrifyingly large, nearly the size of a fucking grapefruit.

"That's not going to fit," I whispered, moving my legs together. Maybe I could ride this mini-heat out with just my own hands. But he kneeled between my legs, pressing them wide, and jacked his swollen erection until hot droplets of pre-cum fell onto my mound.

"You'll take it, baby girl. You'll work so hard for me, won't you? Work to get that beautiful cunt to open up for me? And when you can't get any more in, I'll help you. I'll show you what it means to take your alpha's knot."

A sudden burst of rage welled up in me, and I made that horrifying growling sound again. But this time, I meant it. "You've knotted *other omegas?*" I accused. I knew some alphas didn't think it was any big thing to take a willing omega, even help a friend through a heat. But the idea that *this* man, my alpha, had done this to some other omega before me...

"Shhh," he murmured, stroking my hair as he balanced on his elbows over me, his sweet pine and ozone smell calming me almost as much as his purr. "Not for many years, and never like this. You're all I can see, all I can smell. All I can remember." He set the swollen head of his cock to my opening and pushed in slightly, back and forth, rubbing the slick over him with one hand, while he stared down into my eyes, leaning in for a long, passionate kiss. Then he drew back up and started thrusting deeper.

It burned at first, the stretch barely on this side of pleasurable even though he didn't have his full length inside me yet, and I was still a little scared at the thought of that huge, hard knot battering its way into my body. But he reached down with those clever fingers and started winding my clit up again, working it expertly and humming that purr as he stretched me wide.

"You feel so good, little omega. Smell like custard and berries. I want to stop and suck all that sweet cream out of you, eat what's mine. But first, I'm going to feel you come all around my cock, find out how hard you'll grip me when I—"

His words tipped me over the edge into another orgasm, and he took that moment to thrust the rest of his cock, all except the knot, into me. The combination of intense pressure and unbearable pleasure almost made me black out.

"Touch me now, princess. Touch anything you like now," he purred as he fucked me through that orgasm and began the climb to another one. I scraped my nails down his back, and he began thrusting harder, his knot hammering against my too-small opening each time.

"It's... going to... hurt," I gasped, fighting the orgasm that I knew was coming. I could see in the way he held himself that he was getting close to his own orgasm. He would take that moment, when I came, to split me wide. And a part of me wanted it, *needed* it. I ached inside, burned like someone had set a fire that only he could quench.

"Shush, princess. I'm going to make it so good for you. I'm going to rub your slick all over my knot, and slide it into you so gently... Don't worry, I wouldn't hurt you for anything. Trust me. Open to me. I will take such good care of you. I'll keep you safe, my love."

For some reason, it was that gravelly vow, that he would protect me, which sent me over the edge. I felt my pussy start to flutter in the beginning of what felt like a tsunami of pleasure cresting on the horizon. Felt something give—a band of muscle I hadn't realized had been tight, now loosening a fraction. And then his fingers were everywhere, his teeth scraping the side of my neck.

I threw my head back, exposing my throat. "Claim me, Alpha!" I shouted as I began to come.

"Take this knot, sweet girl," he commanded, still purring, and beginning to thrust even harder. My pussy expanded even more as I was swept into a vortex of sensation. I could feel every inch of that bulging flesh as it pressed inside me, re-shaping and filling me so intensely I wasn't sure if I could breathe. Was it pleasure, or pain, or both? I screamed out my climax as he pushed the last of the massive knot into me, and I felt it swell, growing impossibly larger. Locking us together.

A burning heat began as he started pouring his cum inside me, bathing my walls with his release. "My perfect little omega," he growled in my ear. "Soft and sweet. Gonna fill this hot pussy with my seed, fuck you so deep, knot you so long. Breed your tight little cunt until your belly's full." His wicked promises triggered another orgasm; my walls tightened around his knot, like a fist squeezing him. "That's right, milk me dry, baby girl. You'd better milk it as much as you can, because when I'm done, and you're dripping with my cum, I'm going to flip you over on your front, and I'm going to see how tight that sweet, hot ass of yours is."

He chuckled darkly in my ear when I gasped. He wanted to fuck my ass? How? "I... I never..."

"Never had a cock in that tight hole, sweet girl? I'm sure

you've never had a knot there. I'm going to stretch you so wide, push those soft legs open, lick you everywhere."

I'd never heard anyone talk this way during sex. I'd never even dreamed the things he was suggesting were possible. But I could hear the promise in his words. I knew he was going to wreck me, take me in every way he could. I came again, and again, as his burning hot cum filled me.

He would own me. And I would welcome it.

I felt his hand move over my stomach, cool against my feverish skin as I descended from another shuddering climax. "Look at that beautiful bulge," he said, scraping my lower abdomen with his fingertips. I peered down blurrily. It was slightly distended. My god, how much had he emptied into me? "So full, aren't you? Full of my seed."

Then I felt his knot growing slightly smaller. He thrust a few more times, then slipped out, moving down so that his face was hovering over my pussy. I felt his hands moving around my swollen lips. "What—what are you doing?"

"Pushing it back in, sweetheart," he said, like I'd asked a silly question. When he was satisfied he'd worked enough back into me, he set his knuckles at my entrance—to keep the liquid inside me, I assumed—and pressed his tongue to my engorged clit.

"Wait—" I began, but he sucked it into his mouth and began torturing the bundle of nerves, growling and nibbling, forcing me to come again. It was too much. I writhed on the slick-soaked nest, and felt his knuckles slipping deeper inside me.

"Shush, princess. Hold still. Your poor little pussy already had my knot. I don't think you want my fist in there tonight." His laughter was dark. "I'll have to stretch this tight little cunt for a while before we can try that. But when I do, you'll beg me for it." He sucked my clit again, and I squealed as I felt another knuckle pushing into me.

I had never thought of myself as very sexual, not even after I'd perfumed. I'd never had forbidden fantasies. But this alpha was uncovering a treasure chest full of wickedness. I wanted him to do everything he'd threatened, and more. I wanted to serve him, suck him. Be his good girl, no matter what that meant.

"Claim me, Alpha," I begged, as another orgasm began to barrel toward me. "Bite me."

His fingers still working in and out of my fluttering cunt, he slid upward, his hot skin burning mine as he brought his face to my neck. I felt his short beard and then his teeth against my throat, the sharp points of his canines suddenly sharper. I came, waiting for the bond to form, for the connection between us to create that bridge of love I'd read about in so many novels.

But then he was pulling away. Standing, staring down at me with eyes that glinted with what couldn't have been tears as he said, "I won't, princess. I can't."

"What—" I scrambled to my own feet. The oppressive heat dissipated instantly, and the slick and cum that rolled down my inner thighs felt cold and sticky. "Why not?"

"I'm no good," he murmured, wiping his face. He reached for a shirt, moving as if he would clean up the mess on my body, but I flinched away from his touch. He hung his head, his dark hair shining. "I'm too old. You're too young. I'm not going to steal your future."

"Get out," I snarled. "Thanks for the fuck." He sighed, but as he turned away, I heard crying.

I knew it wasn't him. Was it me?

"Fuck," a baby's voice said from the monitor out in the main bedroom.

"I'll take care of him," Pax told me as he strode out the door, his trousers in one hand. And then there was more crying.

But this time, it was definitely me.

Chapter 9

Candy

The next day, I woke up on the floor of the closet, my heat a distant memory. It wasn't dawn yet, and I had never been more humiliated or angry in my life. Happy fucking birthday to me.

I did a quiet tiptoe of shame down the hall to the nursery and peeked in. Benny was fast asleep, so I crept back to my bathroom, showered all the various dried fluids off my body, washed my hair, and tried to figure out how to burn down a nest without catching the house on fire. I had just gathered the bedding and clothes into a hamper, when I heard Pax clear his throat at the door.

"I'll do that, princess."

"Don't call me that, please," I said, refusing to turn and look. "And I made the mess. I'll take care of it."

"We made the mess together." He walked into the room, grabbing the hamper. He looked... not angry, but tortured. "And we might have made a baby as well." I waited for the punchline, but he didn't go on, just glared down at the laundry.

"You worried I'll try to force you into a marriage?" I tried not to sneer as I said, "Never fear, Mr. 'I Want to Breed This Pussy.' I've had Paxson Pharma's finest triple-shot fertility suppressant. It's impossible for me to get pregnant right now." Of course, if what I'd heard anecdotally about true mates was accurate, an annual heat cycle could break through close to the end of the twelve months. But it couldn't happen yet.

He looked up. "When was your shot? Which one did you take?"

"The annual dose, about two months ago."

"Good. That's good. Then there's no way you could have conceived."

I swiped my face with the back of a hand, wiping off tears. This man didn't deserve them. But I didn't drop my gaze. I let every bit of the scorn, rage, and humiliation he'd inflicted on me show in my eyes. For some reason, he broke off our stare and sank down on the edge of the bed.

"My mother was an omega. She and my dad... they were perfect together. They met, fell in love, and got married the next week. They had me, then Victor, then two more of my brothers, Luke and Teddy. The twins, Lin and Kati. When she got pregnant with the triplets, Mom wasn't well. The girls thrived, but the doctor told Mom not to get pregnant again. Dad got a vasectomy; Mom had an IUD and was on the pill. But it still wasn't enough. Mom died when Penny was four days old, and Dad had a heart attack the hour he lost her."

He stared out the window. "I was about your age. We had all the money we could ever use, thanks to the family business. But in the space of a few hours, we lost the only things we needed. I had an infant to care for. Victor was off at college and said he'd come home, but I made him finish his degree before he returned to help me."

"You didn't have sitters? Nannies?" I knew most families with this sort of money had whole flocks of them.

"The first nanny I hired seemed fine," he said, his voice haunted. "I thought I could go to work. But when I came home unexpectedly one day, she'd left Penny in a dirty diaper, crying, while the bitch took a smoke break for who knows how long."

"That's awful." I wanted to reach out to comfort him, but I knew he didn't want that.

"No, awful was the sitter who tried to abduct the triplets for ransom. After that, I realized the only thing that mattered was my family. So I threw everything I had into raising them as my parents would have. Once they were all in school, I took over running Paxson Pharma again, alongside Victor. I made sure they were safe, and secured their financial futures for the day when I wouldn't be there to help them. I didn't date until Penny was in kindergarten. I never planned to marry, or look for a mate."

"Why not?" I made fists to keep from reaching for him.

He let out a short, dry laugh. "You pick. Seeing my dad die of grief when he lost his true mate? Losing the life I had planned when I became the de facto parent for nine siblings?" His eyes cut to me, and I was astounded at the pain reflected in those bitter chocolate pools. "I was your age when my choices vanished. I may be a complete asshole—no, I *am* one—but I have this much decency left in me. I will not take your choices from you."

"What choices?" I asked, my voice stripped raw. "Mine were already taken."

"They're not now. Not anymore." He stood, placing a sealed envelope on the bed. "Happy birthday, Candy. The roads will be open before nightfall. I've called in some favors to get you home, or to wherever you want to go."

I swallowed, trying to get the words to come out—"*What if I choose you?*"—but all I managed to say was, "You wouldn't have chosen this, would you? Chosen me." I kept my eyes fixed on his back, watching the play of muscles underneath his shirt. He kept flexing, as if he were fighting some invisible foe.

This must be what it looked like to fight the true mate bond.

"You're perfect, princess..." he began. But I knew, no matter what he said now, no matter how he tried to dress it up in platitudes about me having my whole life ahead of me—of how it wasn't me, it was him—the truth of it was clear.

I wasn't enough for him. I was a young, immature, uneducated girl. Not a fit mate at all.

"You don't need to take care of Benjamin," he said softly. "I'll watch him. If you want to come down for lunch..." He trailed off and departed.

I didn't cry when he left. I was numb, and I knew that staying that way was all that might save me.

Sometime around noon, I heard snowplows and trucks. I put my mother's clothes back on and gathered my purse, stuffing the socks I'd missed in my nest deconstruction into the bottom of the bag. I kissed Benny on the head, nodding tersely to Pax as he held the front door wide.

"I'm sorry I wasn't... what you expected," I said stiffly. His eyes dropped to my hands, and I realized I was clutching my tote so tightly that my knuckles were white, to keep from grabbing him.

"You certainly weren't," was all he said, but his eyes were filled with so many emotions, it was hard to tell what he felt.

In an hour, I was home, with my parents fussing and worrying about where I'd run off to. Mom pulled me into a hug. "Anyone could have hurt you, sweetheart!"

"Anyone did," I mumbled into her hand-knitted Christmas sweater. I knew there would be one just like it under the tree for me.

"Want some mulled wine, birthday girl?" Dad called from the den.

"Great idea," I called back, impressed at how normal my voice sounded. If I was lucky, I'd be able to stay numb until I was alone.

Mom pinched my cheek as she went past. "Pale, you look too pale. Come open your birthday presents, then go to bed early, maybe? We're having the Vanderwalls over tomorrow for Christmas!"

I stifled a curse, and went for the wine. A lot of wine. I managed to stay numb for almost twelve hours. Only sixty or so more years to go.

Mulled wine hangovers were brutal.

The only thing worse was throwing up mulled wine at two in the morning after your twenty-fifth birthday, reliving the exact moment your true mate rejected you.

The only thing worse than that was your mom being there, holding your hair back and listening to every detail of the rejection.

I'd had to lock her out of my room to get away from her maternal rage. Migraines and shouting did not go together. At eight a.m., my phone pinged at seven million decibels next to my head. I managed to find it, swiped past the two hundred missed calls and the birthday greetings, and read the only texts that mattered.

Rain: Your mom called. CALL ME

Rain: CALL ME CALL ME

Rain: Your mom told me what happened. I texted Soleil. Let your mom in.

Soleil: Rain texted this morning. I'm coming home.

Rain: Your mom is going to call the fire department to chop down your door.

Soleil: ACK it's Christmas. No flights out until tomorrow. NO DESPAIR ALLOWED

Rain: On my way over.

Rain: I'm outside.

Before I knew what was happening, I'd dragged myself to the door and Rain was in my bedroom, hugging me awkwardly. Rain almost never hugged anyone, so I appreciated the effort. My stomach was sloshing, and my head spinning, and the final bit of the mulled wine numbness wore off in an instant.

"Tell me everything, Candy," she said, and I did. When I was done, she stayed silent for a long moment, then demanded, "Say that last part again." She handed me a glass of orange juice that had appeared somewhere between me telling her about the nest I'd built, and me pulling his dirty socks out of my purse and practically stuffing them into my nostrils.

"The part about not being enough for him?" My nose was so snotty, I could hardly understand myself.

"No. He said he wouldn't take your choices from you. And then he gave you..." Rain fished around in my purse and pulled out the unopened envelope. "Open it."

"I don't want to. I'm sure it's the ten thousand dollars. And if I take it, that's... well, it's not prostitution. But it would *feel* like it. Like my true mate paid me off."

"Fine, I'll open it," she said firmly, using a wickedly long purple nail to slice open the thick, creamy paper. It wasn't a check inside. Well, there was a check, but there were other papers, too. She pulled out a letter and read silently, her dark eyebrows doing some crazy hopping dance.

"What?" I interrupted her facial spasms. "What does it say?" She shushed me and kept reading through the documents. Then she stared up at me, dumbfounded. Rain never looked like that.

"He got your spot back at Sycamore U. On a full ride scholarship, a new one he established for all omegas who present while they're students there. There's also a copy of a formal apology from the Board of Trustees and the University president, and an apartment contract for a three-bedroom apartment right next to campus, and—" I had the envelope and all the papers out of her hands in seconds.

"Holy shit, this is an offer for an internship... a *paid* internship at Paxson Pharma. And if that goes well, I'll be given a spot as a junior exec in charge of philanthropic outreach." I read on while Rain squealed.

"Oh my gosh, it's Pretty Woman minus the debasement! He *does* want to be around you."

I let the paper fall, and the tears as well. "No. It stipulates I have to work on the other side of the country, or internationally. Not here. Not with him."

Rain held me for a while again, then sighed. "I don't get it. Why do all this for you if he didn't feel something? Why go to all this trouble?"

"Guilt?" I muttered, but I was just as confused as her.

Just then, Mom called up the stairs, "Start getting ready, girls!" I lifted an eyebrow at Rain.

"It's Christmas, right?" she reminded me.

I shivered. "Oh, shit. The party with Andreas."

"You're still afraid he's going to ask you to marry him? You don't have to now. You can go back to college, and work, and be who you wanted to be all along."

"Can I?" I sighed and threw the papers on the floor. "Why *not* marry Andreas? At least I know what I'm getting into with him. And he wants me. He's asked often enough. Maybe I should just plug my nose and say yes."

"You can't mean that," she gasped as I dragged myself into the bathroom. "He has a giant booger in his nose at all times, Candy. At. All. Times."

"Could be worse," I called back. "I learned that the hard way this week."

She went quiet for a while, and when I came back into the bedroom to get dressed, she had the little twitch she got in her eyelid that told me she was up to something.

"What are you planning?" I asked. She shrugged, pretending to mess with the makeup at my vanity. "You're not going to cause a scene today, are you? It'll hurt Mom's feelings."

"I would never," she replied, applying some terribly pale eyeshadow too low on her lid.

I grabbed the applicator and did her makeup, then my own, and by the time we were both dressed—Rain in a dress and shoes I'd bought as her Christmas present, since she didn't really have money for frivolous extras—we looked for all the world like two omega socialites who had everything they could ever want.

Andreas floated through the front door on a cloud of alpha pheromones that smelled like a combination of mildew and old tuna salad; it was worse than ever before. It almost made me want to vomit when he came in for a kiss, and I turned my cheek instead. Rain saw my panicked look and took his arm, drawing him away.

"Have you ever had allergies, Andreas?" she asked, wiping at her nose slightly. "I have seasonal ones. It makes my nose run..." She kept him occupied talking about his lifelong battle with cedar and oak pollens, as well as all sorts of molds and grasses, while I chatted with his parents, who I'd always liked. The socializing went on for hours before we sat down to eat, though Rain and my mom carried the conversational load for me.

Before I knew it, dessert was being served with tall flutes of champagne, and Andreas was rising, tapping on his flute with a dessert fork for attention. I wasn't scared, or excited, or anything at all, when he dropped to one knee and opened a velvet ring box, asking me to marry him.

Rain had risen out of her chair and was shaking her head fiercely behind him, though only I was looking her way. "What a beautiful ring," I murmured, taking the box from his hand and staring down at it. He was trembling with excitement, and his scent bloomed around us. I stared into his eyes, trying as hard as I could not to look at the tiny white speck in his vastly wide nostrils. "I'm so honored. It's every omega's dream to marry an alpha like you."

My mom gasped.

My dad let out a soft curse.

And a voice I hadn't thought I would ever hear again growled, "It's not your dream, princess."

Chapter 10

Pax

Not an hour after my little omega had left the morning of Christmas Eve, her shoulders rounded and her head low, Lindyann called. Benjamin was on my office floor, playing with soft blocks, and I put her on speakerphone.

"How's my baby?" she asked immediately. "Did the betasitter work out?"

I couldn't answer her, and to my mortification, when I tried to speak, a sob was all that emerged.

A fucking sob.

"Is Ben okay?" Lin demanded, shouting for her husband to start packing and get a flight while I fought for control.

"He's... fine," I said, my voice stretched thin. "It's not him. It's *her*."

"Her?"

"The betasitter. Not a beta. An omega. She was my true mate." I clenched my hands into fists so tight, I thought they might break, and cut her off when she squealed with happiness. "And I can't ever see her again."

"Tell me everything," Lin ordered.

"I can't," I said truthfully. "I'll lose it completely, and I have to be here for Benjamin."

"I'll be home tomorrow."

"That's Christmas Day, Lin."

"See you soon."

"Don't—" I began, but she'd hung up.

The next day, Lin and Ben Sr. arrived, dressed in tropical attire with winter coats, their faces appropriate for a funeral. Lin kissed Benjamin, then handed him to Ben Sr. and pulled me into my office.

"Jeez, this place is a wreck," she muttered, picking up tissues and whiskey bottles as she made a circuit of the room. Her eyes fell on the trash can, overflowing with crumpled papers and topped with a soiled dish towel, and I blushed.

"Leave it," I grunted, and she nodded.

"Now, tell me." Leading me to the leather loveseat, she pulled over an ottoman so she could sit directly in front of me. "You found your true mate. And she left you? Is she an idiot?"

"No," I replied. "She's your age. Young, with her whole life in front of her."

Lin blinked at me. "And she didn't want you because...?"

I rubbed my hand over my face. "She wanted me. She fucking built a nest in your closet. Went into a mating heat."

Lin growled low at that, paced to the door, and shouted, "Ben! Keep out of my old room!" He yelled back in the affirmative, and she settled back on the ottoman. "And after the heat— I'm assuming you stayed for that—what happened?"

"I didn't bite her, if that's what you're asking. She begged me to, but I couldn't. She deserves better than me. I sent her away with enough money to get back on her feet, enough plans in place. She deserves her choices to be—" I had to stop talking, because Lin slapped me across the face, hard.

"What the *hell*, Lin?"

She was glaring at me with more disgust and rage than I'd ever seen directed my way. "You went into your true mate's nest, fucked her, knotted her, then *dumped her* and sent her home with money, like you could buy her off?"

"It wasn't like that," I protested.

She rose, dark curls bouncing around her reddened face. "You threw away your chance at happiness—you threw away *hers*? For what? Do you know what it does to an omega, to be rejected like that? It empties her out. It makes her life flat and dull. I had a friend who lost fifty pounds and almost died, you asshole."

I sat there, frozen, while she castigated me. Had I done that? Had I harmed Candy in some irreparable way? But I hadn't meant to... I had meant to set her free. Maybe find her again someday in the future. I tried to stand, but staggered as a wave of dizziness flooded me.

"Pax?" Ben Sr.'s concerned voice at the door broke through the fog. He held his son in one arm, and the phone I'd left in the kitchen in the other. "It's been ringing for the last ten minutes. Someone named Rain said Candy's going to get engaged to Booger Nose in an hour if you don't get your ass to Candy's house. She wanted me to say these words: 'You left her no choice.' Is that a corporate espionage code or something?"

Lin pulled me to the door. "Go get your omega, Nicky. And bring her back. I can't wait to meet her."

The fight I'd been waging against my inner nature was lost in an instant. Within a minute, I was in my Range Rover, the snow tires slowing me down slightly. Her parent's home was over an hour away on a clear day. It took an hour and four minutes for me to get there, and another minute to cross the lawn and race through the house.

The place smelled like lasagna and garlic, with undertones of burned custard and mildew, tuna fish, vanilla, and mint. It made me want to vomit. I held still, unsure where they were.

Then I heard her voice, but it was strained. Raspy, as if she'd been crying for hours. Her words came out slowly, hesitantly. "I'm so honored. It's every omega's dream to marry an alpha like you."

Fuck. Was I too late?

I ran toward her voice, down a hallway that led to a dining room filled with a dozen people. Exquisite in a pale pink and gold gown, Candy stood in front of a kneeling alpha who could only be Andreas, holding a ring box in her hand, staring at the gaudy ring inside.

"It's not your dream, princess." My voice was raw as I saw her fingers twitch toward the ring, though her eyes flew to me.

In three steps, I had crossed the room, tipped the alpha onto his back like a turtle, and thrown my omega over my shoulder, to the shouts of everyone at the table. Everyone except for a young woman with a phone lifted in one hand—recording a video, I assumed. She gave me a thumbs up, and I suddenly recognized her from my cyber-stalking.

"Thank you, Rain."

"Who the hell do you think you are?" the sniveling alpha whined. While he demanded I put his fiancée down, I turned to face the only others in the room that mattered. A slight, gray-haired beta couple, who appeared equal parts angry and confused. I'd known they were in their early seventies, but they seemed older.

Her father obviously knew who I was, and what I'd done, because he stepped forward. "You haven't hurt her enough?"

"Mr. Kane, I will never forgive myself for sending Candy back to you, even if I thought she could do better than me." We both glanced at the sputtering alpha on the floor. "But I made that mistake already. I won't make it again. I am your daughter's true mate, Nicholas Paxson, and I would love to have you all over to meet my family soon."

"It's hard for a dead man to throw a party," my omega spat in my ear. I realized then that she'd been beating at my back with her little fists.

I squeezed her tighter, and nodded to the group. "I'm sorry to do this, but I need to apologize to Candy in private. And then spend the rest of my life making it up to her, and taking care of her."

Rain called, "Her room's the second one on the left, just up the stairs!"

"RAIN!" Candy yelled, but we were already in the hall. When I dumped her on her bed, she was still cursing, but her perfume had soaked into me like heated nectar. I knew she was angry, but she was also turned on. Kneeling at the edge of her bed as she sat up, I pushed her legs open.

"What do you think you're doing?" she demanded, but didn't close her legs. I pushed her dress up, revealing a scrap of pink lace covering her mound.

"I'm apologizing," I explained, burying my nose in her cleft, pulling in great lungfuls of her scent. For the first time since yesterday, I stopped trembling.

"You can't just apologize with sex."

"With orgasms," I corrected, pulling the panties down. "Hundreds of orgasms."

She tried to pull her thighs closed, but I growled, and she stopped. "Why?" she asked, her voice filled with pain. I flinched; I'd done that. I'd injured this sweet-hearted young woman.

"I wanted you to have choices," I rasped. "I didn't want to

be the reason your dreams were taken away. Not when I could give them to you."

"Even if it meant you lost your only true mate?" she whispered. My eyes flew to her. She'd known all along, of course. She pressed a hand to her sternum and continued. "When you told me to leave, it felt like my heart was ripped. Physically torn, deep inside. I thought I would die. I almost wanted to."

Her tears might as well have been acid, burning my soul. "I'm so sorry. You deserve a better man than me."

The corners of her lips lifted, even as tears rolled down her cheeks. "Do I? Where would I find one, hm? A man who sacrificed his own youth so that his sisters and brothers could have theirs? Who works himself to the bone to make sure they're provided for, who cooks and cleans and knows how to change a diaper in the dark? One who's so handsome that I can't even look at him without wanting him?"

I swallowed. "I thought... you wanted a choice. I didn't see until it was almost too late that I'd taken your choice away." Her eyes fluttered shut, and my heart skipped a beat. "Forgive me, princess. Claim me, and let me claim you."

Her small fingers covered my mouth as she shook her head. I held my breath. Was she saying no?

She let out a shaky breath. "It wasn't all your fault. I could have told you that I wanted you. You're mine, Pax. And I forgive you."

My heart soared. "You do?"

"Of course." She chewed at her lip. "Though if you still want to give me a few of those 'hundreds of orgasms' you were bragging about, I suppose I can— Ah!" She stopped talking as I drew a thick stripe from her ass to her clit with my tongue. The room was so heady with her perfume now, it coated my lungs with each breath.

"Bragging?" I growled. "I'll show you bragging."

"All talk, old man," she squeaked as I began to suck her clit. "Let me know if you get tired."

"Challenge accepted, princess."

My omega had said I didn't need to apologize, but her body told a different story. I could feel her caution, an ingrained reticence to be hurt again, and as I kissed and licked, nibbled and lapped at her core, I murmured apologies. I wrote them on her with my tongue and lips, learning her body as she shivered with pleasure.

I rode her up to the edge of a climax with just my tongue, then stopped, my eyes fixed on her. "Sit up, Omega," I commanded, and she pushed up on her elbows with a whine.

"Tired already?" She tossed her head. "Top drawer, the big purple one with the knot. It's my favorite."

"The only knot you'll have in you is mine, princess."

Her eyes sparkled. "I don't know, I heard all sorts of promises the last time that didn't happen. All. Talk."

"You're being a very bad girl." I slowly pushed a finger inside her. "You'll get punished if you keep going." Her inner walls clenched so hard around my finger when I made the gentle threat, I knew she liked the idea. "Do you need a punishment, sweetheart?" She shook her head, but I pushed up to the bed and settled there. "Strip, princess. I'm going to spank that ass."

"No!" she whispered. "You're not going to do... *that*. There are people here!"

"Well, they'd better be people with very selective hearing or—" Just then, Christmas music started playing loudly downstairs. "Strip now, princess."

Slowly, she obeyed, and I allowed myself to take in the marvel that was every curve of her body as she revealed it. I shifted, slipped my belt off, and unbuttoned my trousers, freeing my engorged cock.

"Now, come here," I told her, taking her wrist and pulling her over my lap.

"You're still dressed," she noted. I hummed, studying the canvas before me. Mounds of pillowy, soft flesh that made my hands itch to decorate them.

"Spread your legs, princess." Her immediate obedience shook me. "If you ever need me to stop, or slow down, you just tell me." I lifted my hand and gave her right cheek a sharp tap.

She flinched, then relaxed. "That wasn't hard at all."

"Not yet, baby. You've never played this way?" She shook her head, refusing to look up. "Now, I asked you a question. Have you ever been spanked, princess?"

"No," she breathed.

I struck her harder. "Just no?"

"No, *sir*. I haven't done anything but... just licking, and plain sex."

I purred a little bit, practically salivating at the thought of all the games we would play together. I started spanking her just hard enough to set up what I knew were pleasurable vibrations in her core. Her ass began to turn pink as she lifted her bottom.

"You like this, don't you? Like being held down, and spanked. I could make you come from this alone, you know?"

"Yes, sir," she whispered breathlessly. "Harder, *please*."

"What a good girl," I crooned, and did just that, striking her three times on each cheek, making sure the imprints stayed, then I gave three sharp taps to her dripping mound. She arched up in a sudden climax, and I worked my fingers in and out of her pussy while she rode the orgasm down. "I'm going to take you from behind now, princess. Knot your pussy, with my thumb stretching out that little ass. Hands and knees," I ordered, but she twisted around.

Her face was red and flushed, perspiration darkening the

hair at her temples, as she grabbed my hips with one hand and my cock with the other. "Wanna taste," she mumbled as she sucked me into her mouth. Her tongue wrapped around the tip, exploring the smooth head, tracing the veins. I rested my hands on the back of her head and moved her a little lower, not thrusting, but encouraging her to take more in. She was eager and took a little too much, choking slightly. I liked that more than I should, and a thick burst of pre-cum flooded her mouth.

When I lifted her head, her lips came off me with a pop. "My turn, princess," I murmured, positioning her on her hands and knees. "Now present to your alpha."

Something in her knew exactly what I meant. She dropped down to her elbows, her head down, her legs spread. I slid her to the edge of the bed so I could stand, moving my hands across her bright pink cheeks, down to her slick-soaked mound. I kicked off my shoes and stepped out of my trousers, my cock slapping against her ass. The muscles there clenched, and I ran my wet hand over the tight pucker, working the tip of my thumb in and out of her ass rhythmically.

"S-sir, are you going to..."

"I'm going to claim you now, love. I'm going to knot you and bite you. Last chance. If you don't choose this"—I let my thumb fuck her more deeply, swiveling to press against a spot inside her I knew would overwhelm her with sensation—"you tell me *now*."

"Claim me, Alpha," she pleaded, her body shivering with tension and anticipation.

I set the reddened, dripping head of my cock to her pussy, and started thrusting. "Push back, princess. Let me inside," I ordered, still working my thumb in her ass as I fought to make space for my girth within her tight cunt.

"So full..." She obeyed, moving back every time I thrust

forward. I felt the fluttering of her walls as I thrust harder and deeper inside her.

"That's it, good girl. Let this little pussy relax so I can fit inside." After a few more thrusts, with my hand on her hip to keep her close, I withdrew my thumb and bent over, gripping the sheets on both sides of her. I growled into her ear, "Don't come yet, little omega. My knot needs to be inside you when you do. I want to feel you strangle me with your pleasure."

She gasped as her pussy began to widen the barest amount. Desperate to be knotted in her when she came, I fucked her as hard as I dared, watching my thick knot stretch her wide. She was whimpering as she chased her orgasm. I pounded at her opening, feeling it begin to gape just enough, and pushed my knot in, setting my teeth at her neck at the same moment.

"Now *come,* Omega," I commanded, and waited for the first trembling wave of her climax before I bit down, tasting her rich, hot blood in my mouth, and feeling the heat of my seed filling her womb.

In a burst like fireworks going off in my core, I felt the mate-bond connection leading from my soul to hers flare into life.

"Mine," I growled, my mind becoming a savage playground, with only thoughts of fucking, rutting this woman until she couldn't remember any other man than me. Until my scent was so mingled with hers, the whole world would know she was claimed.

Inside her, my knot was so engorged that it wouldn't have been physically possible to separate us, and I felt my soul was just as tied to hers. As I descended into my rutting haze, I struggled to speak. "Do you feel it, princess? Do you feel how we're connected?"

She moaned, beyond words; she'd become a being made of pleasure and sensation, a fresh mating heat overwhelming her as she turned to me with hazy eyes. She pulled my arm close to her face, murmured a word that sounded like, *"Mine,"* and buried her teeth in my forearm.

The connection grew even stronger as her pleasure amplified mine, and mine strengthened and prolonged her climax. My knot swelled back up to full size inside her, starting a new cascade of orgasms within her.

"Yours," I agreed, and started fucking her all over again, proving the truth of it.

Chapter 11

Candy

A t some point that evening, I woke to the gentle sensation of a warm cloth moving over my pussy, and cracked my eyes open. "Alpha?" I croaked, and suddenly a glass of water was at my mouth. I ached and pulsed in my core, feeling liquid rushing out of me as I sat up to drink.

I couldn't remember some of the past few hours, but I knew I needed to call Pax Alpha. Once or twice when I'd used his name, he had taken it as some sort of insult and made me chant "Alpha, Alpha" with every thrust, like some kind of perverted cheerleader with a very simple team name.

My vaj was totally on Team Pax in Rut, though. I wondered how often that happened. Like, omegas had an annual heat, but ruts were sort of on a personal timeline. I'd ask him... once Regular Pax had returned.

"Mate," Rut Pax answered, his dark eyes fixed on my face like I was a treasure. He brushed my tangled hair back, smiling gently as he examined my flushed body, lightly tracing my new mating mark. It sent a shower of tingles to my clit and a wave of warmth to my heart at the same time. "All fucking mine."

"Wow..." I tried not to blush as I returned his stare. He'd gotten completely undressed at some point, and in the brighter light of my room, I could really take in his body. The lines of his muscles were as sharp as his jawline, and the dusting of dark hair that was sprinkled on his chest led down to a cock that, even flaccid, was thick. I trailed my fingers down his muscles, mapping them out, then stroked his cock, making it stir again.

But he closed his hand around mine, stopping the motion. I peered up at his face, but his eyes were moving around the room, taking in the pink and yellow accents, the dresser covered with both makeup and stuffed animals, the shelf of dance trophies I'd never bothered to get rid of, and the pictures of me from high school—a slightly pimply teenager with six of my friends in ball gowns at prom—as well as the one of me, Rain, and Soleil at our first charity outing with the Omega League.

"You're so young," Pax murmured, and my stomach churned. I put a hand on my neck. No, I was pretty sure it had been his stomach that churned. "This room..."

"Old enough to be claimed," I protested lightly.

"Hell, my brothers are never going to let me hear the end of this." He swung his legs over the side of the bed, staring at the shelf of my favorite plushies next to my vanity table.

My heart constricted. "Omegas like soft things," I found myself explaining, then stopped.

"I know, sweetheart," Pax said gently, but the mate mark still felt peculiar.

A sudden voice at the closed door called out, "Um, girl-friend? What are the signs of a heart attack? Because if you two don't come out soon, your dad's going to have one."

"Oh my god." Wrapping the sheet around me, I ran to the door and opened it a tiny crack. "Is everyone still here? Could you... You could *hear* us?" My voice ended on a whispered squeal.

Rain was backing away, wafting the air from her face. "Oh my god, did you guys start a perfume factory in there?" Her eyes were gleaming, and she wiggled her eyebrows up and down at me. "So?"

I forced a smile and wiggled my own eyebrows up and down, opening the door just wide enough for my neck to show. She grinned, with only a hint of sadness in her expression as she gave me a double thumbs up.

"Seriously, though, you two need to get downstairs. Everyone's been gone for hours, except me and your folks. Andreas left in a *huff*. His parents stuck around for some of the show, though. Come down as soon as you can."

I nodded and shut the door, turning to find Pax gone, along with his clothes. When I heard the shower, I realized he was already in the en suite bathroom.

This wasn't how it was supposed to go. Sure, I'd claimed Pax and he'd claimed me... but the way he'd left the room, and me, without a word? It felt... odd. I quickly straightened up the bed, then rummaged in my closet for a clean dress.

When the bathroom door opened, I still looked like I'd been fucked twelve ways to Sunday, but Pax looked like a put-together billionaire businessman as he adjusted his gold and black onyx cufflinks.

He shot me a tight smile. "I'm going to have to apologize to your parents."

"Yep," I replied, moving past him to the bathroom. He dropped a kiss on my head as I went past. "I've decided just to never look my dad in the eye again. And move away."

"Move in with me?" He stopped me, grabbing one of my hands. "Tonight. Come home with me, and you can get started on your new life."

I felt the unmistakable presence of a *what the actual fuck* scream stuck in my throat, and swallowed it down. "My new life?"

He nodded, then grabbed his phone off my dresser, scrolling and typing as he answered. "You may be my mate now, but that doesn't mean I took away your dreams. You've got that job offer at Paxson Pharma starting in January. You could get settled in at my house this week, then we'll go to Telluride so you can meet my family." His eyebrow twitched slightly at that. "Do you still want to finish your degree? Or just skip it and go to work? No, you can do both, if you'd like. A work-study position, with time for instruction in the afternoons..."

He wasn't asking me anything, I suddenly realized. I wasn't sure he was even aware I was in the room.

"How about getting married?" I stepped in front of him, forcing him to look at me. "That's normally what people do after..." I put a hand to my mate mark.

"There's no rush," he murmured, but his nostrils flared as he took in my naked state. A burst of his pine and ozone scent swept over me.

I stroked his cheek, shivering at the rasp of his short beard on my hand. It felt almost as good as it had on my thighs. "But we will, right? Get married."

"If you want to," he replied after a moment, his gaze intense. "But I know you had plans, dreams. So what's important is for you to have those back, no matter if that means school, or work, or travel..."

"Or having babies?" I interrupted. "I know that might be hard, but I've always wanted children eventually."

He nodded, somberly. "Since Mom's death, I've spent the last two decades finding pregnancy-related treatments and procedures to help omegas. I've used my fortune to improve surgical outcomes, and to make fertility suppressants that work, even with true mates. Whenever you decide you want children, I'll support that, too."

He would *support* that. Not *want* it.

Every insecurity I'd felt since meeting him surged to the forefront of my mind. So Pax didn't necessarily want kids with me, but he wouldn't complain.

I swallowed hard, hoping I was reading too much into his word choice, but deeply worried that I was not. "Even though you raised your siblings?"

His smile was tight. "Of course. By the way, I'm not sure my sisters will ever stop teasing me about mating the betasitter." He reached into his pocket and pulled out a tiny, etched metal box. "Not unless I make it official."

"Is that...?"

"It is," he said, his eyes soft now. "There's no rush, but I'd love for you to wear this."

My fingers shaking, I snapped open the box. I knew without asking that this had been his mother's ring. The brilliant-cut diamond wasn't huge, but it was an unusual blue-white, and etched on the sides of the ring were unmistakable shapes... "Candies?" I asked, wondering at the coincidence. "Are those really candies on this ring?"

"Dad always called Mom his sweetness. She smelled like peppermint and taffy. So he had this ring made." His eyes shone. "It seems like fate. I took it out of my safe on Christmas Eve." He cupped my chin in one hand, gazing into my face with fierce emotion. "Will you be mine, my sweet Candy?"

"Yes," I replied, trying to sound calm as he slipped the ring over my knuckle. It didn't quite fit, sliding loosely around my finger.

But I was determined to make it work.

Chapter 12

Candy

The morning after Christmas, I woke in my fiancé's king-sized bed to the press of a rock-hard cock against my back. "Still sleepy?" Pax murmured. On the bedside table, his phone was vibrating over and over, but he ignored it.

I took that as a good sign. He had admitted on the drive over that he worked too much, but had promised to try to do better.

He'd made that promise to my mom, too, when she shocked us all the evening before by ripping Pax a new one when we came down from my room.

"About time," Mom muttered from her chair as Pax and I entered the living room. Dad just raised an eyebrow. Rain had already taken off, giving Pax the stink eye and me a pat on my shoulder and a promise to call, saying she had a gig. She couldn't mean a betasitting one at this hour, and I didn't know what other job she could have, but I let it go.

Dad had a crystal tumbler of whiskey in his hand, and Mom was pretending to read a magazine. I almost lost it when I real-

ized she was holding the copy of Alpha Roll *that Soleil had bought me as a gag gift. The cover had* "Omega Orgasms and How to Prolong the Pleasure with Plastic (Sex Toys)" *and* "Alpha Bachelors Worth Drowning For" *with a picture of a frowning alpha on an enormous yacht.*

"Mr. and Mrs. Kane? I didn't properly introduce myself earlier, and I'm sor—" *Pax began, then stopped. I had to stifle a giggle. He wasn't really going to apologize for having wild sex with me for the last few hours, was he?*

But his eyes were on the mate mark on my neck. Wait, he wasn't going to apologize for claiming me, was he?

But he finished, "I'm sorry I burst in on your Christmas celebrations."

"No, you're not," *Mom mumbled. She glared at him, and I cringed, remembering all the details I'd shared with her the night before, when I thought I'd been a rejected mate.*

Dad was merciful and merely nodded. "Can we get you a drink?"

"Please."

Mom shot out of her chair to grab Pax a whiskey, frowning slightly as she passed me, until she noticed the ring. I held up my hand with a smile.

Pax approached my dad. "Sir, I know I didn't ask you for your daughter's hand—"

"Good. It's not 1850, and he doesn't own me," *I grumbled, though the laws about omegas meant my designation more or less lived in the legal Dark Ages.*

"Nicholas," *Dad said, ignoring me.* "You do go by Nicholas?"

"Please, call me Pax. Or Nicky. My family uses that."

"Nicky. I like it." *Dad took a sip of whiskey.* "You're not wet behind the ears like the other alphas who've come sniffing around. I think you might be a good match for our Candy. Tell me about your family, and your business."

"The third degree, Dad? Really?" I complained, as Mom walked back in.

Dad let out a huff. "Well, this is all rather sudden."

"I agree, sir," Pax replied. "But that's how it often is with true mates. My own parents were scent matches, true mates, and they met and got married within a week."

"Your mother will be glad to hear that," Dad murmured to me. "The woman's obsessed with those bride shows."

Mom cleared her throat. "I'd rather hear why Mr. Paxson here met his true mate and rejected her. I'd like to know why he made her sick all night with—"

"Sick?" Pax was looking down at me, checking for signs of fever, before Mom had finished her complaint. "Are you sick, love? Why didn't you tell me?"

I shot Mom a glare. "I'm not sick. I did throw up, but to be fair, that was the mulled wine."

Pax visibly relaxed, but Mom kept staring. "I still haven't heard an answer. Why did you hurt my baby?"

He faced her, his cheeks darkening with what looked like shame and regret. "I have no excuse. I was just trying to protect her."

"Protect her from what?" Mom demanded, her voice belligerent. I recognized the tone: cross-examination of a hostile witness.

Pax didn't look away from Mom. "From losing her dreams. You know she wanted to graduate from college, work in corporate philanthropy?"

"Of course we knew. But things changed... when she changed."

"And they can change again," he said. "She can have the future she dreamed of, and more. I've already lined everything up. I'm going to give her everything she ever wanted, Mrs. Kane."

"Marta. And we'll see," Mom replied coolly, but she handed him the drink. "Have a seat, Mr. Paxson. I have some more questions for you."

"You're trusting me to take care of your daughter. You can ask me anything."

I winced as Mom continued to interrogate Pax. "You hired a nanny to watch your own nephew instead of taking care of him yourself. I'm not impressed, Mr. Paxson. If my daughter does marry you, are you willing to give her the attention she needs?"

"I'll still be running Paxson Pharma, Marta. I may not be with her every hour of every day, but I will make time for her. And she'll be busy as well, chasing those dreams at my company—"

"Not that I've decided exactly what I'll be doing—" I began, but Pax cut me off.

"Of course, she may still choose to finish her degree. It's all up to her. I assume you're the one who taught her to value philanthropy? That was one of the things about Candy that impressed me the most. Her values are solid."

Oh, he was slick. Mom melted like a snowflake on a hot stove. Then he went one further, and asked her about her favorite charity, Caritas.

"Marta, I made a donation to the soup kitchen this week, after I saw you sat on the board. They do amazing work."

"Wait, you're the anonymous donor?" Mom practically screeched. When he nodded, she looked like she might pass out. "Ten million... You met our funding stretch goal for the decade. Thank you, Nicky."

She'd finally called him Nicky. Pax grinned like he'd won the lottery.

My heart melted a little, too, when he smiled at me and said,

"I know how important philanthropy is to Candy. And she's the most important thing in my life now."

Maybe I'd been worried for nothing. He'd seemed kind of cold, like he'd taken off his "claimed Alpha" suit when he'd put on his Tom Ford businessman clothing.

And maybe he'd more or less left me to my own devices the night before, but an important call had come in just after midnight, and he'd vanished into his office while I got ready for bed.

Once Pax had come to bed, he'd spent another hour showing just how happy I made him, and from the way he was caressing me now, he had plans for a long day in bed, getting to know one another.

I didn't hate the idea at all.

"Sleepy? I'll stop." His lips vibrated with a purr on my neck as his hands wandered over my naked curves.

"Not that sleepy."

"Then hold still," he commanded. I did, and let him move me, parting my legs, his cock entering my already wet entrance slightly, his fingers wrapping around me and teasing my clit until my slick coated him. I tried to turn and reach for him, but he chuckled. "Hold still, and let me fuck you." His left arm came up and around my neck, wrapping around my throat gently as he began to thrust into me. "Such a good girl, opening for your alpha. Does it feel good?"

"Yes," I whispered, the pleasure already spiraling. "It always feels good with you."

"It always will."

As he made soft, slow love to me—the orgasms he gave me cascading softly over each other, like a snowfall of bliss—the whole room filled with our mingled scent, a blend of strawberries and pine. I breathed it in as his knot slid home, purring at the warmth of him along my back, his hands gentle on my hips.

His own purr rumbled from his throat, and I knew I'd never heard such a beautiful sound.

When he was done, I almost fell asleep with his knot inside me, as the soft, steady brush of fingers in my hair, gently moving the strands behind one ear, lulled me toward dreamland again.

"I've decided that's my favorite feeling in the world," I mumbled into the pillow.

"What is? My knot inside you?" Pax chuckled, thrusting gently, which made his knot move just enough to start another tiny series of pulses inside me.

I shook my head.

"My fingers on your clit?"

"Not that either."

He grunted. "My hand on your neck?"

"No, *sir*. Not that either." I giggled.

"Laughing at me? Do you need another spanking, brat?"

His grip on my ass almost had me saying yes. I wondered why I'd never known how fun a thorough, not-too-intense spanking could be. I felt the sudden urge to text Rain and Soleil and share my thoughts, but that seemed like very bad etiquette.

Sex etiquette was the sort of thing the League should teach us omegas. I could almost hear one of the older omega guest speakers admonishing the group. "Polite omegas allow their alpha's knot to subside before calling friends to chat about new kinks and positions. One thing at a time, ladies."

"What is it you love most, then?" Pax murmured.

"Your hands in my hair," I admitted. "When you touch me like this, it makes me feel... cherished."

"I want to cherish you." He nuzzled my neck, his short beard scraping my sensitive skin deliciously, but then he sighed. "Unfortunately, I have a conference call this morning."

Huh. I'd never known the words "conference call" could work as well as a cold shower.

If he vanished into his office all day like he had last night, I wouldn't get the chance to talk to him about what was on my mind. Namely, the way he'd started making decisions for me. Like what I'd told him last week I wanted in my life was still the same, even though we were mated now.

The situation was different now, as if my perspective had shifted completely. Sure, I wanted to work and maybe even finish school, but my inner omega needed something more: security.

So I gathered my courage, held up my hand where his mother's ring hung loosely on my fourth finger, and cleared my throat. "Do you think we could set a date? Plan for when we'll tie the... *knot?*" I asked, squeezing him inside me. He let out a groan of pleasure, and I sent up a silent prayer of thanks to the Goddess of Kegels.

When he could speak again, he answered, "Whenever you want."

"Wait. Whenever? Like, in a year, or in... a few days?" I tried not to squeak, but couldn't help it. My heart was suddenly racing.

He went still. "Oh, not that soon. I'm sure you'll need time to plan."

"Oh. Of course." I wasn't about to admit I had a Pinterest board with every detail of fourteen separate dream weddings planned out, along with potential inspo bridegrooms. Well, Henry Cavill and Tom Hiddleston and a few others, but those were my pre-Paxson ideals. I'd need to replace their pics with him.

"Your mother seemed pretty set on getting you married, even to someone clearly inappropriate."

"You mean Andreas?" I smothered a giggle at the unmerited jealousy in Pax's voice.

"That was the pathetic little alpha's man's name, yes. Andreas Vanderwall III." Every syllable dripped with disdain. "Weak-chinned, narrow shoulders, watery eyes. I'll have to see if he wants to participate in a clinical trial for a new testosterone booster." Then he grumbled something about bedwetting and internet porn addiction.

"After you sweet-talked her, Mom probably already started planning the..." I almost said *baby nursery*, but didn't want to freak Pax out entirely. Mom's greatest dream was to see me settled down and popping out grandkids, like a human-sized gumball machine.

"Just remember, there's no rush," Pax insisted, his knot shrinking as the combined topics of Booger Nose and my mother did their work.

His phone began vibrating on the table yet again. "Who's calling so much?"

"My PA or Dr. Murray, most likely."

"Wait, a doctor? Are you sick?"

"Paxson Pharma, remember? Dr. Murray is a genius, our top research scientist. Degrees from Cornell, Johns Hopkins... Truly a great mind. Anyway, there are some very worrying things going on," he murmured as he rolled out of bed.

"What kind of worrying?" He hesitated before picking up his phone, looking torn between answering it or me. "Pax, it's okay. I don't need details. Just big stuff, huh?"

"Very big. Life-or-death big, I'm afraid. But I'll get it all sorted out." His voice trailed off as he checked the phone. "Ah, no. This one's from Lin, Benjamin's mother. She knows work has blown up for me, and wants me to get you on a plane to Colorado early. They're all desperate to meet you."

"Right." I swallowed hard. "Time to meet the future in-laws."

He grinned, and I was suddenly breathless at how handsome my mate was. "They'll love you. We always try to ring in the New Year together at Paxson Lodge, in Telluride. All ten of us, plus any spouses or significant others—that's only Ben Senior and you this year—and a small staff."

"Sounds fun," I lied. "Our first vacation together as mates. Should I get some gifts for them?" But he was already in the bathroom, the shower running.

Billionaires probably didn't need presents. But everyone loved cookies.

And stress baking was a time-honored tradition in the Kane household. I knew exactly what I was going to do today while Pax worked.

Chapter 13

Pax

I scratched at my forearm where Candy's mating bite was burning again. Well, not a burn. More of a sensation of light pressure, or pulsing. It had started yesterday—the morning after we'd come back home—and was getting more pronounced by the hour.

I'd never heard of a mating bite getting infected, but something was wrong with mine.

Not that I had time to deal with physical pain. One of my head researchers was coming by this morning to share an extremely concerning report and discuss our response to it.

Somehow, omegas in New York and New Jersey were experiencing heats, even though they'd been prescribed Paxson Pharma's flagship product, our combined fertility and heat suppressant. I was almost certain there was something wrong with a batch of the drug, but there was always the outside chance that some omegas had developed a resistance to the drug. Before I met with the board, I needed to speak to the only person who would know.

And while she was here, I would ask about the clinical

trials of the alpha hormone suppressant that my friend Storm had been taking.

"Pax?" Candy's voice came from the doorway to my office. The day before, she and Chef Adaline had gotten into some sort of argument, with Candy wanting to bake something, and Adaline insisting that she was happy to make the pastries, or whatever.

When I'd tried to explain to Candy that she didn't need to make her own sweets, she got angry for some reason, and stormed off. I'd tried to placate her—I'd told her I knew young omegas were emotional; it was understandable—but that had just pissed her off even more.

I took a deep breath before I looked up from my laptop. "Yes, princess?" I had to fight the surge of pure lust that always threatened to drag me under every time I saw her.

And then the answering surge of remorse. How fast I'd gone from swearing I'd move slowly, to biting her and taking her away from her life and her home. I made a mental note to follow up with my PA on that junior executive position we were creating for her.

She looked even younger than twenty-five today, with her dark hair up in a high ponytail and no make-up at all, just smooth skin slightly flushed from exertion. She looked incredibly youthful from the neck up, but she was wearing some sort of exercise clothing that was molded to her form like a second skin, and from the neck down she was every man's wet dream.

"Slick and juicy?" I growled as I rose from my desk, reading the words plastered across her chest aloud. She moved toward me as well, as if we were being drawn together by invisible forces. "Is that a request, or—"

"Hello?" A sharp rapping sound at the doorway had me stopping just short of grabbing Candy, and she whirled around.

"I'm sorry, have I come at a bad time? I thought our meeting was now?"

"No, it's fine, Saryn," I replied, smiling perfunctorily at my colleague before moving quickly behind my desk to hide the erection currently tenting my trousers. "Please come in and have a seat."

"Well, hi there," Candy said with a wide smile. A wide, *fake* smile.

"I'm Dr. Murray," Saryn replied, shaking Candy's hand while I desperately tried to think of dead skunks and financial audits. "And you... Oh, I know! You must be Penny! I knew Paxson still had one little sister living at home. Aren't you graduating from high school next year? What an exciting time for you!"

Candy froze in place. I felt my cheeks heat, which made me inexplicably angry.

I had no reason to be embarrassed. But I'd never thought about Candy's reaction to being with me. Did she feel awkward standing beside an older man?

Would it look creepy for me to embrace her in public?

"No, Saryn." I stood back up, returning to Candy's side. "This is Candy Kane, my, ah, my..."

"His betasitter," Candy finished, her voice as sharp as Chef Adaline's best knives and colder than the weather outside. "He hired me to watch over little Benjamin."

"Oh, how embarrassing!" Saryn shook her head and laughed. "Staff gets younger and younger. I really am sorry. Could you please bring in some tea, then? It's so chilly out today."

Candy's eyes cut to my face, and my life flashed before my eyes. Or, more specifically, my death. Which would be soon and incredibly painful if I didn't correct Saryn's assumption.

"Saryn," I said, then stopped when Candy shifted away

slightly. "I mean, Dr. Murray, this is my mate. My true mate, Candace Kane." I put an arm around Candy, the one with my mate mark, but for the first time, the contact wasn't soothing. It felt... dangerous.

"Oh, wait," Candy said, her voice saccharine. "Is this the Dr. Murray you told me about? The one who went to Cornell and Johns Hopkins and—"

Saryn laughed. "He's been bragging about me? That's so gratifying. He hasn't said a word about you to anyone."

Somehow, Candy went even more stiff under my arm.

"It's very new," I began. I'd been so swamped, I hadn't even thought about telling my colleagues, or the press. Saryn had an NDA, but I'd need to talk to Candy, and to my siblings as well, about how we wanted to go forward.

As soon as the crisis at Paxson Pharma was over, I'd figure out how we would weave Candy into the family as well as the company. I'd need to get her security set up before anyone knew—

"Pax?" Candy murmured, breaking into my thoughts as she moved away from me. "You've got this meeting, and so much going on. I know my mom has been missing me, and I haven't seen my friends for a while. Maybe I'll just... head home. That sound okay?" Her voice was brittle.

My vision flickered with traces of red. No, it was not fucking okay. I wanted her in our bed at night. I needed her arms around me in the morning, every morning for the rest of our lives, and more than that. I wanted her to be by my side every day as I worked. I wanted to throw every fucking one of my responsibilities away and immerse myself in the miracle that was my mate—

"Oh, you still live with your parents? Paxson, you cradle robber! I'm starting to see why you kept this to yourself." Saryn's laughter interrupted my sudden, insane urge to drag

Candy into our bedroom and bite her a few more times, so she'd remember she was mine. Keeping her to myself sounded like a great idea. Tying her up until she begged me never to let her go. The mate mark on my arm flared with heat.

Fuck. Was I still in rut?

I leaned down and whispered, "Are you sure you don't want to stay? You're welcome to listen in on the meeting. You can sit on my lap."

"Oh no, I wouldn't dare interrupt the grown-ups at work," she hissed back.

I sighed. "Candy—"

But she was already on her way out.

Chapter 14

Candy

The brilliant-cut, blue-white diamond ring on my left hand, etched on both sides with tiny candy shapes, felt heavier for some reason. Just like my heart did.

I shouldn't feel sad; I should feel blissful. Lucky. I'd won the freaking omega lottery.

"I did, didn't I?" I asked Rain. "I won the omega lottery, right?"

She'd just arrived in the middle of my packing frenzy. Pax had texted me that his siblings wanted me to come out to Telluride as early as possible.

I hadn't mentioned that to Rain yet. Or Dr. Murray. Or why I had turned Pax's notifications off on my phone until I knew I wouldn't cuss him out if I heard his stupid voice.

"From what I can tell, you may as well have won an actual lottery. Your alpha is loaded. He probably shits gold bricks into his gold toilets. Speaking of smelly shit, it *still* stinks in here."

Rain wandered across my bedroom, one hand over her face now, muttering about the stench. Apparently, Pax and I had "permanently destroyed" the room on Christmas, and the residual perfume of our lovemaking, even days later, was so thick it was clogging her lungs.

She threw open the window and stuck her head out. "Yes, bitch, you won the lottery. You're the brand-new fiancée of one of the richest men in the world, who is also unfairly hot."

I sighed and picked up my e-tablet. "I know that. Everybody knows that. Did you see the article in *Alpha Roll* magazine a few years back, where a bunch of women threw actual panties at him?"

Rain hmphed. "Apparently, an acceptable flirting technique for alpha chasers."

"I know!" I'd been doing a deep internet dive on his personal life since I'd left his house. Partly to understand him, and partly to see if what Dr. Murray—the surprisingly gorgeous blonde beta, who was so educated and intelligent and renowned it made me want to tear her hair out at the roots— had said was true.

Had he really told no one about us?

Was he ashamed of me, and keeping it a secret?

I wanted to think it was just shitty timing. Apparently, the constant buzzing on his phone on Christmas night and the day after had been something awful going down at Paxson Pharma. When he'd finally checked his messages, he'd vanished into his home office and spent almost every hour there.

"He's not just sexy and rich and ridiculously good in bed, Rain. He's responsible, kind, hardworking, and generous. He raised his nine younger siblings after their parents died. He built his family's company into—"

She interrupted my monologue. "This is sounding an awful lot like that time you tried to convince yourself bangs would work on you, me, and Soleil. You made a spreadsheet of reasons we should all enter hairstyle hell."

"This is nothing like that," I lied. "I wish Soleil had come back from St. Croix. At least she always says something cheerful." Of my two besties, Rain was the pragmatic one, and Soleil, the optimist. It balanced out most of the time.

"I can be cheerful." She twisted around to face me and bared her teeth. "See? Smiling. Now tell me what the asshole did."

"It's stupid."

"Candy. Dresses without pockets are stupid. Decaf coffee is stupid. Doing the cinnamon challenge in gym class is really, really stupid. And except for that last one, you are not and have never been stupid."

"Hey, I got out of eighth grade gym class for a month doing that challenge," I protested, though she was right. I still felt sick if I tried to eat a cinnamon roll.

I scratched at my neck, my mate mark burning again.

"How long has that been hurting?" she asked, then looked around my room. "When did you come back here?"

"A couple of nights ago."

She sucked in a breath. "Oh, shit. You broke up?"

"Ah, no. Come on, we can spend time apart. We're not codependent. Yet."

"You're biologically dependent, Candy. You're scratching at your neck like you've got fleas. It's making you itchy to be apart from him."

"It's probably just a rash."

She narrowed her eyes. "What did he do?"

I crumpled. "Where do I start?"

"How about with why all your clothes are on the floor?" She gestured to the piles along the walls and the open suitcases.

"I'm packing. For our first vacation ever."

"Yeah. New Year's Eve with the future in-laws, the reason you told Soleil not to come home early from the Caribbean. Which I'm still mad about. With you and her both gone, my

New Year is gonna suck donkey balls. When is he picking you up? Today, tomorrow?"

I couldn't look at her. "I'm not sure he is picking me up. I think he's sending me on ahead." After she let out a string of expletives so loud my mom yelled up the stairs for us to turn down the television, I finished, "By myself, while he hangs out with hot lady doctors and hides the fact that I even exist."

Rain grabbed both my hands in hers. "Tell me."

Once I started, I couldn't stop. I told Rain everything: how he'd changed almost immediately after we'd claimed each other. How he'd been too busy to talk, which made it all that much harder to be mated to a stranger.

"An old, soon-to-be-dead stranger," Rain muttered. "Go on."

"And then this doctor came to the house, and she was his age, but super hot, you know? Unfairly thin and elegant, smart, with perfect clothes, and when she asked who I was, he got awkward about it. He hasn't told anyone, and I'm not sure he's going to." I knew I was being slightly dramatic, but sometimes emotional exaggeration was a girl's best friend.

"What. The. Actual..." Rain stopped for a calming breath. She held up a finger and closed her eyes, pressing her other hand to her diaphragm.

I knew what that meant. Rain had anger management issues, and even though she'd taken every meditation, yoga, and emotional health course our local Omega League offered, she just got madder and madder as the years passed. Her latest online therapist was big on using a certain pattern of breathing to calm down.

While I waited for her to finish her pattern, I thought about the Omega Bride subscription that Mom had just sent me on my tablet, and wondered if I'd even need a wedding dress. My eyes stung with tears.

Huh. Maybe I needed to try the breathing.

When I sniffled, Rain stopped trying to breathe peacefully and started pacing, all five feet no inches of her bristling with rage.

I sat on the edge of the bed. "I think he regrets claiming me."

She made a weird growling noise. "That's not possible. What was the doctor's name again?"

I told her, and she looked it up on her phone. "Aw, hell. She's practically Margot Robbie with a PhD in molecular biochemistry. Thank goodness she's a beta... and *not his true mate.*" She rolled her eyes at me. "And he still wants you to go meet his family, right?"

"I suppose. He texted me and said if I wanted to start planning my future wedding, his sister Kati would help." It had kind of surprised me to hear his rich sister was a wedding planner. But I guess even billionaire betas needed something to fill their days.

Rain blinked. "Wait. You said he was sending you *on your own*, to meet his horde of siblings?" I threw her my phone and let her read his texts. "Holy shit—your wedding? He honest to god calls it *your* wedding."

"Yeah," I said slowly, definitely needing the breathing now. Of Pax's nine siblings, eight would be at the lodge. Meeting the future in-laws was hard enough. Meeting them alone? Terrified me more than a little. "I'm sure he meant *our* wedding."

"Sure. Slip of the thumb," she muttered. "Old people suck at tech."

"He's a CEO. He doesn't suck."

"Wait. Are you telling me he doesn't go diving?" She pointed to her crotch, as if I didn't know exactly what she meant.

I rolled my eyes. "No, Rain. He's all about the breakfast in bed." I managed to laugh. "I didn't know a woman could get sore from too much oral, Rain. The man is insatiable."

"Damnit, you make it hard for me to want to murder him, Candy. An alpha who eats pink breakfast tacos in bed? Those aren't all that common."

I knew that; at the Omega League, we even had a name for alphas who didn't snack down south. We called them Uptown Men, sometimes in front of their faces. They thought it was a compliment about their social status, but it was really omega code for "selfish lover."

"Sex isn't the problem, Rain. I'm just not sure he really wanted a mate. Or at least, not one like me. I think he's having second thoughts. I keep wondering if he's looking for a way out."

"There is no way out," she said ominously. "I would know."

I had to stop myself from apologizing to Rain, for bringing up what had to be the worst possible memories.

She had encountered her true mate on vacation when she was much younger, and he'd rejected her flat out. She never talked about it, and I was pretty sure only Soleil and I even knew it had happened.

Her smile was sad and fleeting. "Listen, Candy, if that fucker can't see how miraculously amazing you are, if he doesn't understand that you're the main attraction of his entire life, his fated mate queen, then he doesn't deserve you."

"Like you said, it's a little late now. It's not like I can take him back for a billion-dollar refund."

Her dark eyes narrowed as she handed my phone back and got hers out. "No, you can't. But I can take him *down*, Candy. I know a lot of ways to make an alpha disappear. Even one his size."

"Disappear?" I swallowed hard.

"You think I've learned nothing in all my years of watching

true crime shows? All it takes is planning, a solid alibi, and a pig farm if we can find one." She began tapping on her phone. "Give me a minute. Gotta use an untraceable VPN..."

"I don't want to feed my true mate to pigs!" I blurted out. "I just want him to love me enough that he'll tell people, that even if his family h-hates me—" I stopped talking and stuck my chin out, trying to forestall the tears I could feel coming.

Gah! Why was I this emotional? I counted back the months since my twelve-month fertility and heat suppressant shot. I wasn't due to turn into an emotional wreck for at least ten more months, give or take. Was this what a mate bond did to an omega? Turned her into a basket case?

"What if I'm not enough for him?"

"Candy, Nicholas Paxson is a lot of things, but he's not a fool. He's gonna have you locked down and popping out tiny heirs to his billions within a year."

"But why would he be ignoring me now? This is supposed to be the honeymoon phase, right? Why would he even think sending me off ahead would be okay? I know work's bad, but... am I mated to a man who won't put me first?" I whispered aloud, wondering if I'd made a mistake. A terrible, emotionally crushing mistake.

"A mistake? All alphas are mistakes."

Ugh, I'd said that part out loud? Of course I had. "Not helpful, Rainy Day."

She lifted one narrow, dark brow. "But true." She rubbed my shoulder awkwardly. "If he doesn't end up loving you with every ounce of his being, Candy Kane, he's the biggest fool ever. And I *will* feed his dead alpha corpse to pigs if he hurts you. I already told him that, more or less."

Damnit. The words "if he doesn't love you" hit me right in the hormones. I wiped away a tear as Rain sat next to me, her own eyes wide, like I'd done something terrifying.

"There, there," she said, patting my hand. "No crying or I'll have a panic attack. You know that." I struggled to control myself, knowing it was true. Rain might not have a lot of emotional intelligence, but she more than made up for it with loyalty, honesty, and dark humor.

"Candy, will it make you feel more in control of your emotions if I let you help me research local pig farms? Or should I just do it quietly, so you can rest?"

"Don't feed my fiancé to pigs, Rain," I sniffled.

"Fine," she grumbled, patting my hand a few more times. "If you change your mind, just say the word."

"What word?"

Her eyes sparkled with humor. "Hmm. How about *grapefruit?*"

I fell back on my bed. "I should never have told you about his knot," I wheezed once I'd stopped laughing. "It's not actually that big. I mean... a small grapefruit, maybe. Like, a navel orange? Not one of those pomelos or anything."

"Listen, if an alpha comes at me with half of a baseball bat, and a softball-sized knot at the end of it, I'm running. I don't care if he smells like Chez Palette on dark chocolate raspberry croissant baking day. I want to keep my intestines where they are, and my cervix unperforated, thank you very much." She shivered, waving a hand down her tiny frame. "That shit won't fit."

"We're omegas, Rain," I teased, more than happy at the topic she'd chosen to pull me out of my mood. "We're literally made for alpha cock and knots." I smiled, remembering my alpha's knot. "And breakfast in bed."

A huge waft of strawberries and cream filled the air around us.

"For crying out loud, Candy." Rolling off the bed, Rain ran

for the window again. "You're going to make me puke. When's your next heat cycle, anyway?"

"I got my twelve-month shot in October."

"That's right. Maybe your intense odor is a mated omega thing." She stuck her head out the window, overdramatically gasping for air. "I don't know if I'll ever be able to eat a strawberry tart again."

"Sorry. I'll try to stop thinking about it."

She craned her neck back. "I'm just jealous. Lucky bitch."

I sighed. "I know I'm lucky. I just wish we were together."

"He'd better pull his head out of his ass, soon. He doesn't have time to waste, what with his advanced old age."

"He's about to turn forty, Rain," I snapped back. "Not four hundred."

"You say potato, I say tomato. You're his true mate. He should be on you like white on rice."

"I'll go back to his place tonight, and maybe we can talk it out."

"I have a better idea," she said, an evil smile curling her lips. "Let's go to a club. Send him a few pics of you looking like... well, you. If he doesn't come running, I'll owe you a Bestie Favor."

"You're on." I laughed as she held up a dress that was pretty much eighteen square inches of gold sequins held together with mesh and happy thoughts. "What if he doesn't, Rain?"

"Then, I'm telling ya, I will take steps to make sure he never hurts my bestie again. Pig steps." She went back to packing, muttering something that sounded like, "They even eat the bones. The *bones*."

I ignored her and took a deep breath, counting for a long moment.

And then I put on the damned sequins.

Chapter 15

Candy

"This is amazing!" I shouted to one of the Omega League women dancing next to me. We'd somehow skipped the entire line at $lick, the hottest club in all of Georgetown. Getting in here took either a two-month wait, or a lot of money, or fame, or all three. We'd just walked in, after Trina had tapped the bouncer on the shoulder, then spoken privately to the club manager. He'd escorted us inside, but not until he'd taken some pics of all five of us: me, Rain, Trina, and two of Trina's friends.

Trina wasn't a friend, exactly. But she always knew where the best parties were, and lived a "more the merrier" philosophy, on the streets and in the sheets, if rumors were to be believed.

And by rumors, I meant the pictures on her phone she'd proudly displayed to all of us an hour before of her with three alphas at once. It had kind of turned my stomach, but Rain had seemed intrigued.

Rain had texted Pax a picture of us outside the club, and I

knew he'd be here any minute. But I was going to enjoy myself before he got here.

And then maybe I'd get another spanking tonight.

"Trina, I can't believe we got in here. How did you manage that?" I shouted over the deafening beat.

The flashing lights on the dance floor painted Trina's face red, blue, yellow, and purple, but the green of envy shone clearly through when she shouted back, "Are you kidding? Of course we got in. You're wearing Nicholas Paxson's marks on your neck. That's all Marco needed to hear."

"Marco?"

"Yeah, that's my neighbor, the club manager. He popped a pic up on the club socials, hope that was okay!" I gave a blurry thumbs up. I'd had a little too many of a new cocktail the beta bartender had called "Sweet and Numb," but for the first time in days, my mate mark wasn't itching or burning, and my mind was blissfully empty.

I closed my eyes and lifted my hands in the air, knowing my sequin dress was centimeters away from showing off the tiny thong underwear I'd put on. Every once in a while, a hand slid over my skin, but I danced away. I was only here for one alpha.

The best thing about this club was the high-powered air filtration system. I took a deep breath in, amazed that I could be surrounded by so many others, including alphas, and not be overwhelmed by the scents. "I love this place!" Behind my closed lids, the lights flashed over and over, almost like a strobe.

"*Fuck.*" Rain's shouted curse had me opening my eyes. She stood with her hands up in front of my face, like she was trying to stop something from hitting me. None of the other omegas were around, though the dance floor was more crowded than ever, so for all I knew they were nearby.

That's when I saw the cameras. Cameras? Why were there a dozen gross-looking guys with cameras all over the dance floor? And one down on his knees, angling a shot up at my... "Pervert!" I yelled, kicking him over with one of my heels. His camera went sliding across the dance floor.

"Paparazzi," Rain yelled in my ear, her hands pulling me away from the dance floor. "Trina is such a bitch."

"Trina?" I asked, though it was really hard to say her name. "She called the paps? Why?" Rain's face went yellow, blue, red, purple, then pale, as she stared at something behind me.

"Because you're my mate, Candace."

"Pax?" I spun around too fast, losing my balance, and landed in Pax's arms. "You came! Let's dance."

"Let's not." He shot a dirty glare at Rain, then looked back at me, his face a mask of color-changing disappointment. "Time to go home, sober up, and then we'll talk about this little stunt."

"No." I pulled away from him, or tried to. He didn't let go, and started taking off with me. "No! I'm not going home."

"No, you're going to my home, where you'll stay until we leave for Colorado."

"Fuck you." The words were spoken before I could stop them, though I slapped a hand over my mouth right after they came flying out.

"What did you say?"

I was hazily aware of a line of security guards heading our way, and the cameras still flashing. But the "Sweet and Numb" drinks had done their job, and the disdain on Pax's face was too much to bear.

"Just leave me here. I'm not going to your house either. You're mad, and you're just going to force me to sit alone in your stupid house while you sit around with stupid Margot Robbie doctor ladies, and do your stupid work." I waved a hand around, and somehow it landed on Rain. "You tell him, Rain. You love me. Not like him. He doesn't love me; he doesn't even like me. He wishes I'd never knocked on his door."

"I don't," Pax said, clenching his jaw.

"See?" I said, my heart tearing into tiny pieces. "He admits it."

"That's not what I said, baby." He wrapped one arm around my waist, the other somehow scooping under my knees.

"Let me down! Let me down!" I kicked and struggled, but it was no use. He was bigger and older and meaner than me. "Let me down! I don't want to be your true mate, Nicholas Paxson!"

Unfortunately, the music had stopped right then, and my words were all anyone heard.

"Fuuuuuuuuuuuck." Somehow, Trina and her friends were standing right in front of us. One of them had her phone out, recording everything. The cameras were still flashing, but no one near us said a single word.

They were all watching the train wreck of my life.

Pax flinched, closed his eyes like I'd stabbed him, then kept going, shooting quiet orders to the guards.

"Paulo? Take Miss Torres home. Anthony? See if you can buy up the paps."

"Won't happen, Mr. Paxson."

Pax nodded. "Just try." He wouldn't look down at me, not when we got to the car, not even when it started heading toward Southeastern Georgetown.

A call from his PA came in. "Mr. Paxson? The online tabloids are already hitting."

Pax rubbed his forehead. "How bad?"

"'Billionaire Alpha Abducts Unwilling Young Omega.'"

"Shit. That bad?"

"That's the best one, sir. They have recordings of her struggling to get away, fresh mate marks showing. They blurred out her exposed... nether regions, but—"

"Stop!" The PA stopped talking when Nicholas barked the word. "Get them all down. No matter what it takes." After a few more moments, Pax hung up and slumped back on the seat, his head hanging.

"I didn't mean it," I whispered, and finally, he looked at me. I'd seen a lot of emotions in his eyes in the short time I'd known him. But this was something new, and terrible. It was... devastation.

"Are you sure, princess?" When I opened my mouth to answer, he held up a hand. "I told you I wouldn't take away your choices. Where do you want to go right now—my house or yours? Where do you want to sleep it off?"

"Where will you be sleeping?" I asked, feeling like I might be sick.

"I won't be. I'll be doing cleanup with the press, then going to an early morning meeting with my board."

That was all he needed to say. "Take me to my house."

"I didn't like him for you at first," Mom said softly the next day. She and Dad had called in sick to work. Mom said it was to support me. Dad said he was afraid he'd go on a rampage and kill everyone who'd seen my nearly-bare ass on the internet. Apparently, one of his co-workers had forwarded him a link asking if I'd really been abducted. My aunt had sent a "thoughts and prayers" email letting him know her whole church was praying for me to find Jesus, or a more appropriate wardrobe, or both.

He'd literally deleted her number off his phone.

Honestly, none of us could get out of the driveway since paparazzi had surrounded our house. It wasn't a fancy gated subdivision like Soleil lived in—though she'd texted from St. Croix and said her parents had invited us to hole up there—so we'd had to close all the blinds and curtains.

Mom rubbed my shoulders gently. "The first time he made you cry, I wanted to smack him. This time, it's your turn to reach out, honey. You claimed him right back, and that means you're going to be together forever. Talk it out, explain how you're feeling, what you're thinking. Spend time—"

"How?" I asked, my voice raspy. "He's busy with work, and I'm trying to be understanding. But he doesn't let me in. He won't talk to me about it, just says the most annoying shit about young omegas *being emotional!*" My sentence ended on a screech, and Mom raised one eyebrow. "Okay, and also this stupid mate mark has turned me into a nutcase. I'm just... not sure he even wants me."

"He gave you his mother's ring, Candy," she said softly.

"Well, he didn't tell his friends or colleagues about me. He doesn't want to marry me until I'm older, or maybe better at something. The ring doesn't even fit."

It didn't. It was so easy to take off, and I did that now. But then I put it right back on.

A horn honked outside, and I heard shouts from the press at the same moment Mom's phone rang. I'd turned mine off, since the press had somehow gotten my number.

Mom answered and spoke softly to whoever it was. When she hung up, she hugged me, then grabbed the suitcases I'd packed and carried them to the side door, by the garage.

"Pax's siblings have invited you to go to Colorado today. If the press dies down, your dad and I will stay home. If not, he'll put us up in the Four Seasons Mid-Georgetown."

"I don't want to go. They'll hate me. They'll have seen the stories..."

"They'll understand. They know their brother, and they will love you when they meet you. Everyone does. Be brave, sweetheart. I'll see you in a week, okay?"

Dad came out of the living room just in time to add, "And if you need us sooner, all you have to do is call. You're still our baby, you know."

Tears, hugs, and an extremely burly Alpha guard and driver—both obviously dosed with a lot of scent blockers—filled the next few moments.

And then I was on my way. Alone again.

I scratched the mate mark at my neck until it bled, then pressed a cloth to it in the overheated limousine all the way to the private airstrip.

Chapter 16

Pax

I *don't want to be your true mate, Nicholas Paxson!* The words Candy had shouted at me echoed like the tolling of a funeral bell as I sat in my office, alone.

Well, not really alone. My phone kept me company with its persistent buzzing. I turned it to silent and scrolled down the numbers and texts, hoping to see one from her.

Then realizing I wouldn't. My number was protected, but hers wouldn't be. I shot a text to my PA Theodore, asking him to make sure a new secure phone was sent to Telluride as soon as possible. I tried to think of anything else I could do to keep Candy safe, but nothing came to mind. Storm Security had a full contingent of security at her parents' house now, though they had their hands full.

Of course, she hadn't been protected in that club. A chill rushed through me as I thought of what could have happened if anyone had known. They could have taken her, hurt her... and I would have been to blame.

I don't want to be your true mate, Nicholas Paxson!

They said the truth hurt, but I hadn't known it could cut as painfully as a knife, right into my soul. Of course she didn't want me. I hadn't intended to claim her for this very reason. Candy wanted what any young woman would. Nights at clubs like that one, dancing, and fun. A man who had time for that sort of thing, no responsibilities.

I couldn't remember the last time I'd stopped working for long enough to have fun. No, I could.

It was when the snowstorm had locked my mate in this house with me, and she'd welcomed me into her improvised nest, forcing me to see what had been missing. Joy. Passion. Another word lingered in the back of my mind, but I refused to think it.

Love wasn't something that came easily to someone like me. But with her, it had seemed like it might appear more quickly than I'd ever thought possible.

I hadn't been able to sleep the night before, and I'd mumbled my way through an emergency board meeting that was supposed to be about our response to the crisis at Paxson Pharma, but had ended up being a referendum on my love life.

For once, it wasn't just my workaholic tendencies keeping me tied to my desk. Hundreds of the shots that suppressed omega fertility cycles for one month had been mislabeled as one-year doses, and sent out to doctors' offices. The doses in question had been sent to New York and New Jersey, but it was possible they'd gone to other states as well. We still didn't know if it was an honest mistake, or corporate sabotage. Plenty of old-school alphas didn't believe omegas should have control over their reproductive lives, even though my company had made regulating fertility possible.

Which meant that now, there could be unsuspecting omegas out there in danger of becoming pregnant. Omegas like my mom, who had died because her body couldn't handle the stress of bearing her tenth child, and omega biology was stronger than any birth control drugs available back then.

I rubbed at my arm again, musing at how little was truly known about omegas and their biology. Since Christmas evening, in between panicked meetings, I'd done an hour or two of research on true mate connections, to see if there was any information about irritated mating marks.

There wasn't much information about true mate bites available anywhere, not even in the secure files in my company's research arm. Probably because there were so few mated pairs, couples who were perfect scent matches.

I don't want to be your true mate, Nicholas Paxson!

My heart constricted. The mere thought that my perfect, young mate regretted having tied herself to me, might not want to be with me ever again, had my inner alpha roaring to go to her side and make certain she knew whose she was. To stake my claim all over again, all over her delectable body.

My phone rang, and I took the call, recognizing the ring tone. "Luke, how are things going at the lodge?" I knew Candy wouldn't get there for another few hours; my PA had let me know the instant she'd gotten in the car to the airstrip, and had made sure she had fresh flowers on board the plane with a note from me.

"Get your ass out here, Nicky, or you won't have nine siblings, because I'll bury at least three of them in a snowbank."

"The triplets giving you trouble?" Vanessa, Tori, and Valentine were twenty years old, and if I didn't know they had round-the-clock bodyguards assigned to them, I would be worried. But ever since an ex-nanny had tried to abduct them for ransom when they were ten, I'd paid the exorbitant fees to Storm Security for their very best men to keep them safe.

"I found two ski instructors hiding in their bedroom closet."

"They got into our lodge? How?" With all that security...

Luke snorted. "Two of the triplets snuck them in while the third hit the guards with her—what do they call it? Oh, yeah. 'Omega phasers, set to stun.' Nicky, I need you."

"You need me to hide the bodies, or pay off the hitmen?" I sighed as Luke bitched about the other girls being bad influences on Penny. "Don't they have enough to do to stay out of trouble? Isn't Kati assigning jobs to all of you?" Our oldest sister was the most organized sibling of us all, and was terrifyingly competent.

"Kati is a tyrant, and she's been going without sleep to get everything ready to welcome your mystery omega, but even Captain Kati's no match for the triplets and Penny. Not now that Penny's decided since she's almost seventeen, she's old enough to—and I quote—'step into adulthood with a heart full of courage and a fist full of condoms.'"

"Condoms?" I felt a headache begin to pound at my temples. "What the *hell*, Luke? What's going on out there?"

His laugh was higher-pitched than usual. Hysterical, almost. "The snowpack is incredible. Every resort is sold out, and every fraternity in America, plus most of the world's nouveau riche Eurotrash Casanovas, have descended on Telluride."

"Fuck."

The line went silent. "Hey, I hate to bring it up, but the girls saw some trash tabloid stuff online. Is everything okay with your omega? Are you okay?"

"You heard what she said, right? Let's just hope my family can convince her to stay with me."

"Why the hell aren't you on that plane with her, Nicky?" When I explained what was going on at the company, he whistled low. "I get it, bro. I'll tell the girls we need to impress the heck out of her, talk up your positives. Pretty sure she's already seen your caveman side. We'll keep her safe for you until....?"

"I'll be there tomorrow. Candy's plane is landing in two hours. Nobody runs her off, got it?"

Luke laughed, but the sound was hollow. "I'll try. Don't wait too long unless you're giving her one last chance to back out."

I growled into the phone, "I already claimed her, asshole. There's no backing out now."

"Good. Man, true mate, huh? You deserve the fairy tale. Tell her what's going on at work; she'll understand."

His words stopped me. Would Candy even want to know all the details about the crisis at work? I'd thought it would be boring. But maybe it would help if she knew how serious it was. "Yeah, I just need to get some time with her, get to know her. Let her get to know me. I can't... I can't lose her, Luke."

We both went quiet, and I knew he was thinking of the same person I was. The one Paxson sibling who wouldn't be there. The brother who'd fled to South America months ago, trying to heal from the horror of watching his true mate marry another alpha.

"Any word from Victor?" Luke asked.

"Not yet," I replied, my heart heavy. "But I'm not giving up." I wouldn't give up on him.

I hung up the phone and closed my eyes, allowing myself the luxury of thinking of my new, gorgeous mate. I already knew my family would love Candy. She was smart, funny, open, and kind... and so sexy it made my balls ache to think of having to wait even one more night to feel her wet heat around me, to hear her soft cries as I lavished her body with bliss.

She might not want to be mated to me now, but I had a feeling I could change her mind. I'd apologized with orgasms once before, and I could do it again. I'd start with her on her back, her legs wrapped tighter than a scarf around my neck...

I was distracted from my daydream when my phone pinged. It was a picture from Lin, who'd purchased what looked like matching polar bear outfits, all lying on a bed. I counted the ears, and realized there were at least a dozen of the ridiculous onesies, in all sizes.

Lin: LOOK.

What the hell are those for?

Her reply was short and ominous.

Lin: Family New Year's photo shoot!

Her following texts proved that Luke had already shared my instructions. Lindyann was ridiculously excited to help welcome Candy to the family, but she also sent a warning text.

Lin: Omegas need to be shown how much they're loved. Step up your game. Get your ass here.

Resolute, I made a dozen calls trying to stave off a stock crash for my company and tamp down the media feeding frenzy about the "omega abduction ring" I was apparently heading up, while simultaneously making sure the doctors and pharmacies of any affected omegas would be notified immediately and discreetly about the mislabeling. Then I sent at least seventy-five texts lining everything up so I wouldn't be needed at work for a few days.

Finally, I headed for the door. It was time to meet with the board, and get the results of our internal investigations.

Hours later, I stalked out of the boardroom, anger warring with impatience. The mislabeling had been human error, an accident on the part of a new employee who had mistakenly thought his job was one he could do while simultaneously playing a video game on his watch.

His manager had also mistakenly believed there was no way anyone making base-level pay could screw things up too badly.

They'd both been wrong, and were now fired, with NDAs in place to make sure they stayed quiet until we decided how to share the results of our investigation publicly, now that we knew what had happened.

What should have been a one-hour discussion on how to own up to our issues with internal oversight, had turned into a five-hour hand-wringing session. I'd almost cursed out the entire board, and ended the day by walking out of the meeting.

God, I needed to fall asleep next to Candy. And wake up next to her.

My phone buzzed as I strode toward the front door of Paxson Pharma's main office, and I saw my PA's name. Perfect timing. "Theodore, make sure the Gulfstream's ready and waiting. I've got to get to Telluride tonight." I nodded to the doorman, who used his key card to open the large glass door.

"Your plane is taking you to Dallas, sir," Theodore replied. "And it's morning already."

I stopped walking. "You're fired." The doorman sputtered. "No, not you." I pointed to the phone. "Him."

Over the phone, my PA sighed dramatically. "That makes three times this week, Mr. Paxson. Please let me explain. I had your pilot submit an alternate flight plan when Mr. Storm of Storm Security called. He said to check your email, and that he knew you would want to go to Colorado by way of Dallas."

I hung up and immediately opened the email account that only Storm Halder and his employee Estefan Morales knew about, while the cold December wind raced through the open door. My heart leaped, then fell. I wasn't going to make it to Colorado for New Year's Eve, but I hoped, when I told Candy why, she would forgive me.

If this was true, that is.

I started to text Candy, then had to apologize to my PA to get her new number.

> Sweetheart, I need to talk to you when you wake up. I'll be late arriving.

The text was sent, but not read, and I checked the time as I slid into my car, nodding my thanks to my driver. Of course she wasn't up yet. It was two in the morning in Colorado, already New Year's Eve. I went ahead and sent a slew of texts and voice messages, explaining everything that had been happening with the mislabeling debacle. I debated telling her about Victor, but I knew that would be a complicated explanation, and since I hadn't even told my siblings that he might be joining us, I let it go. More important was giving my true mate insights into what had distracted me from what should have been my primary focus. Her.

And giving her a peek into who I was, besides a businessman.

By the end of the trip to the airstrip, I'd devolved into sharing my favorite childhood memories, interspersed with shorter texts and favorite memes that my younger siblings had sent me over the years.

I'd never sent a woman this many messages in my life. Candy was either going to forgive me, delete me from her contacts, or have me committed. I finished by sending her one last short text, giving her a recap of my delay and my ETA in Telluride.

My mate mark itched relentlessly on the flight, as I reread the emails I'd received from the private investigator I'd hired months ago to do nothing but look for my brother. A week ago, Estefan had reported he had a line on a possible sighting of Victor. In his latest message, he'd attached a grainy picture of a man who looked like my brother in a market in Santiago.

At least, I thought it was Victor. It looked something like him, holding hands with a heavily pregnant woman. This man had a ragged beard, though, and his shoulders seemed narrower than Victor's.

I stared at it, trying to zoom in to see details. If Estefan's information was right, Victor was flying into Dallas in just a few hours. Before I got out of the car and into my Gulfstream, I sent a short email to the PI, with one question: *Are you certain it's him?*

His reply was immediate. *It's him.*

My heart raced.

Victor was coming home, though there was no telling if or when he would leave again. And no telling what shape he'd be in when he got here. Would he be half feral, or dying, as most alphas who lost their true mates were?

I couldn't tell the others, not yet. If he slipped away from me again, like he had all year, it would devastate the girls.

No, I would meet him in Dallas, and then I'd take him with me to Telluride. I was going to make certain he was with our family, where he belonged, on New Year's. Then, we would figure out how to keep him here.

Chapter 17

Candy

The day before New Year's Eve, I stepped off Pax's private plane—or one of them, at least—alone, the frigid air stealing my breath as a trio of gorgeous young women came rushing across the tarmac to greet me. Behind them, three hulking men, obviously bodyguards, scanned the area around a waiting luxury Humvee, their eyes shaded by dark sunglasses. My own security had left me on the plane with a flight attendant who'd clearly never missed arm day, and two pilots who looked like mercenaries, but I was glad to see these new guys.

The paparazzi had been intense, knocking my parents' mailbox down as they chased us down the driveway.

But facing the press seemed easy next to Pax's family. I pulled the hood of my downy coat around my face, hoping these women wouldn't mention my swollen eyes or red face. For once, I hadn't been crying, but some idiot had put an enormous bouquet of flowers in the small airplane, including some sort of yellow clusters of daisies that I was allergic to. The flight attendant had bagged them up, but the air was already pollen-laced, and I'd spent the flight wiping my nose until the Benadryl kicked in.

I probably looked like I'd spent the day crying, but at least I could breathe through my nose again.

As the three dark-haired girls circled me, clad in matching white downy jackets, pink fuzzy hats, and scowls, I forced a cheerful smile. "Hey. Are you Pax's sisters?" My nose was still a little stuffed up, and I sounded sick. *Nice first impression, Candy. Hi, I'm your future sister-in-law, here to infect you.*

"Yes, we are," one of them replied, before gasping. "Have you been crying?"

Another one added, "If it's about the viral TikTok video, I am all over it. It'll be yesterday's news by tomorrow."

"Um, okay..." I was suddenly very glad I'd turned my phone off.

"Why didn't Nicky come with you? You two aren't still in a fight, are you?"

"He's coming as soon as he can get away," I hedged.

"W-were you crying?" the third one asked softly, handing me a tissue. "Didn't Nicky apologize?"

I smiled my thanks. "No, that's not why—there were these flowers... Anyway, I'm Candy—" I couldn't say anything else, because I was suddenly being crushed to death.

Well, maybe not to death. But hugged within an inch of my life, anyway.

"We're Vanessa," one announced.

Then another, still hugging me, mumbled into my neck, "And Victoria. But call me Tori."

The last one pushed her sisters away and finished, "And V-Valentine."

I sucked in a breath and realized that while her sisters were betas, Valentine was an omega like me. As she hugged me, I could make out the vague scent of a Christmas candle, all cinnamon and vanilla, with faint notes of her brother's pine.

"How c-c-could he send you here alone?" she stammered quietly. She took a breath, obviously trying to control her stutter, then let it out slowly. "W-what happened at that c-club?"

"He's coming tomorrow," I explained. "He promised. Something came up at work, though, and you know how it is." It was really hard to keep smiling when her face creased with sorrow for me.

"Yeah, we know about the work thing. Such a mess, right? Scary." I didn't want to admit that I had no idea what was going on, so I just nodded.

Within a minute, I was being force-cuddled in the back of the Hummer, while one of the bodyguards loaded my suitcases in the trunk, and the other two slid into the front seat. They were all alphas, and I almost wished my nose was still clogged. Other than Pax, alphas had never smelled all that great to me. For some reason, two of these three smelled aggressively bad, like a sewage treatment plant staffed by skunks. The driver just stunk like wet wool, though.

Valentine didn't seem to mind, as she kept leaning forward toward the driver and inhaling through her nose until he snarled at her to put on a seatbelt.

Almost before the door was shut, the girls started telling me all about the lodge and what they'd been up to, giving me the details on what to expect over the next few days. "So you know Nicky is the oldest"—Vanessa held up a hand, ticking her siblings off on her fingers—"then Luke, then Teddy. They're all in their thirties, so we call them the Olds. Then there's Lindyann and Kati; they're twins, but Kati's a beta and Lin's an omega. She's Benjamin's mom."

"Is Benjamin going to be here?" I asked, perking up. "I miss that little guy."

"Yep," Vanessa replied. "And it's hilarious. Every time he learns a new word, he repeats it a thousand times. Did you know Nicky taught him to say *fuck*?"

I choked back a laugh. I did know that. "Really?"

She nodded quickly. "We've been taking videos of him wandering around saying fuck and fuck it, dressed up like one of Santa's elves. Once we upload them, he'll go viral."

"You will *not* upload them," the driver muttered without turning his head.

"Yes, Daddy," Vanessa sassed. "*Family* viral, not internet viral. Sheesh."

Tori took over. "Anyway. Then there's us; we're twenty. Penny is the youngest. She's sixteen and—this is going to be so weird—you know she still lives at your house, right?"

I flashed back to Dr. Margot Robbie and gritted my teeth. "Yes."

"Cool. So once we're all back to real life after the lodge holiday, she's going to be living in the house with you and Nicky." She wiggled her eyebrows. "You might want to move her into my room. It's farther from the main suite."

"Uh, I haven't moved in yet," I said, scratching at my neck as the mark burned. "I... I don't know what Pax will want."

The vehicle went dead silent, until Valentine's soft question popped the quiet bubble. "You c-can't think Nicky d-doesn't want you t-to move in. You're his t-true mate. Tori?"

"On it," Tori said, texting furiously. "I'll tell him to get his sorry ass here now."

"It's inexcusable, Candy. Nothing is more important than your mate," Vanessa added.

I shrugged, as Tori held up her phone. "Girls, we're going to need to do a fraternal head-ass-ectomy. He says, get this: 'Can't make tonight. Will try for tomorrow morning.'" She started typing furiously again. "I'll try to kick his nuts up to his larynx when I see him."

Valentine took my warm hand in her cool one. "He'd b-be here if it w-wasn't an emergency."

"I know. It's a huge issue. Life or death." I didn't really know anything, except the amazing Dr. Murray was helping him with it. I stared out the window and did my little chin-jutting trick to keep any tears from starting up. "He'll be here as soon as he can. And until then, I'll get to know all of you. So tell me, what are your weird family Christmas traditions?"

Tori and Vanessa ran with the subject change, and in moments, we were laughing as the Hummer wound its way up increasingly narrow, snow-lined roads to an enormous wood and stone fortress of a ski lodge. Valentine held my hand the whole way, even after we got out of the Hummer, and I loved her for it more than a little.

We climbed the steps hand in hand and entered the lodge, stopping to take it in while her sisters raced off to their rooms. Apparently, the others were busy somewhere else in the lodge, or running late coming in from the crowded slopes. A valet came and whisked my luggage away to a room down one long hall. In seconds, it was only us and Valentine's bodyguard, who lurked in a corner.

The main room had thirty-foot vaulted ceilings, with hand-painted gold-leaf pine cones on the raw wood. The furniture was all oversized, as if we'd walked into a giant's home. A roaring fire crackled on one side of the room, and the scent of burning piñon wood, like honey and smoke, perfumed the place.

As Valentine helped me out of my coat, then hung it along with my giant purse on a coat rack made out of antlers, I took in the art. Oversized paintings and photographs of the family members covered the walls alongside masterpieces by famous

American artists, with a few children's scribbled crayon draw-
ings framed and displayed right alongside them. I found myself
smiling, even though my heart still ached.

"Nap or f-food?" Valentine asked. "I can m-make you something. I'm not a g-great c-cook, though." From the corner of my
eye, I saw her bodyguard's face soften slightly.

"I'm starved," I told her. My stomach growled as loud as an
alpha, and she giggled. "Where's everyone else?" I asked as we
moved toward a door that I assumed led to the kitchen. "Is
there a big meet-up?"

"At d-dinner." She pushed the door open, and a waft of
rosemary and garlic-scented air rushed out. "We'd planned for
you and N-Nicky..."

I tried to joke. "Wow, smell that. The heck with Pax, I'll
marry whoever's cooking."

A man's voice answered from inside the room. "Then it's
my lucky day. Nicky will probably try to kill me, but it'll be
worth it. My god, you're stunning, new little sister."

I spun around, taking in the Pax lookalike who was wearing
jeans, a thermal shirt, and an apron that said *Luke, I am your
Daddy* but inexplicably had a picture of Henry Cavill dressed
as a Jedi knight on it.

"Are you Luke or Teddy?" I asked, as he held out a hand for
me to shake, then dropped a kiss on the top of mine instead. I
blushed as he looked up at me, batting his eyelashes. His face
was narrower than Pax's, and his shoulders less broad. From his
subdued scent, he was definitely a beta. But he was still easily
in the top ten most handsome men I'd ever met, and it made me
slightly tongue-tied.

He grinned up at me with nothing but friendliness in his
gaze. And mischief. "Luke. Teddy's a little younger than me,
but far less attractive. Try not to let him know you think that,
though. He's a very delicate flower."

142

"I'll delicate flower your ass," a loud voice shouted from the doorway. A man who looked like the lumberjack version of my mate came clomping in the door, carrying a huge stack of firewood on one shoulder. "You left me to carry it all in myself, you lazy a—aaahhh, you must be the lovely Candy." The lumberjack stopped mid-curse and nodded, a slight blush covering the tops of his cheeks. "I'm Teddy."

"Hi." Valentine was muffling laughter as we took in the state of her older brother, who had tiny sticks and pine needles in his hair, and snow all over, caking his snow boots. "Need some help?" Luke had his hands full, doing something with a tray of roasted vegetables on top of an old-fashioned Aga stove. I hopped up, ready to help him.

"Omega, sit down," he replied, looking deeply offended.

I took a breath, realizing Teddy was an alpha, though he had the mildest scent I'd ever come across. Like leaf mulch and coffee grounds.

He peered around the room, like someone might be hiding in the corner. "Where's that idiot brother of mine?"

Off to one side, I glimpsed Valentine drawing a finger across her neck in an unmistakable signal for him to shut up.

"What?" Teddy asked aloud. "What happened?"

My cheeks blazed with fire as I moved toward the door. "Nobody told you? There was a... thing with the press. I needed to get out of town. Pax is coming tomorrow."

"Yeah, asshole," Luke said, clearing his throat. "Remember? I told you about the club thing. And the problems at Pharma. He couldn't get away."

"I didn't know Nicky was so full of shi—sugar." Teddy scowled. "Not here because of work? Nothing's more important than... Well, we'll take good care of you, little sister."

Luke's expression held more than a little sympathy. "We will. Val, let's get her fed."

Suddenly, all the love Pax's siblings were showing felt stifling. The room was too warm, my head still fuzzy from the Benadryl, and I wasn't sure if I could look one more person in the eye and pretend I was fine with being here without my alpha.

"You know what, Valentine? I think maybe not food first. I'm so tired. I... I'd like to see my bedroom now."

She nodded and grabbed my hand with a smile, pulling me out the door. I held it together as she escorted me across the main room again, then down an adjoining hallway. The scent of pine and ozone wafted out of an open door. Pax's scent. I noticed a large king-sized bed in the room, but we passed it by. She opened a door to a smaller bedroom, with a queen-sized bed and a view of the mountains. The wall was all windows, and I felt completely exposed.

The sheets smelled clean, almost sterile. A door that led to what I assumed was a bathroom was on one side, a huge walnut armoire taking up most of the opposite wall. There was a small basket of granola, juice, and bottled waters on a side table, and some pamphlets about the area. It was very obviously a guest room.

Set up for one person.

"This is where I'm staying?" I asked, pressing a hand to my stomach, where a constant, churning cramp was starting. Valentine hovered right outside the door. Her eyes met mine, and I was shocked to see tears in them. "Why?" I whispered. "I'm not going to be in the same..." Were they old-fashioned about marriage? My mind spun, trying to find an explanation for the too-small bed.

She frowned. "It's not like that. P-Pax's room had a leak. The c-crew will have it fixed in no time, but Kati said this one has the b-best view. It really d-does."

"Oh." I didn't care about that. I needed his scent. No, I needed *him*.

"Hang on!" She ran out the door, and was back in seconds with a pillow. It smelled slightly of mildew, but mostly of my alpha. Of course another omega would understand.

I smiled. "Thank you."

I held the pillow to my face, the faint scent calming me, until Valentine spoke again. "They d-don't understand. You b-being here, like this. It's a m-mistake."

My stomach lurched. "A mistake?"

She nodded. "A huge one. W-we all know it."

She thought her brother was making a mistake? Meeting me, marrying me?

They all know it? My blood turned to ice. I hadn't even met all of them. What if they didn't want me here?

What if Pax didn't?

My mate mark burned and throbbed like it was infected, but I didn't let myself scratch it while Valentine was watching.

"Good to know," I whispered. I shut the door behind her, locked it, and sat on the bed, watching the snow fall outside the huge picture window for a while. Then, I gathered up every blanket on the bed, the extra down comforters in the armoire, and the pillow with his scent, and piled them all into the bath-tub. It was a nest, sort of. But the saddest, smallest, loneliest one that any omega had ever built.

With the lights out, I fell asleep buried deep in the soft fabric, wishing I was anywhere but here.

Chapter 18

Candy

The next morning, on New Year's Eve, I dragged myself out of the tub, brushed my teeth, got dressed in the lightest clothes I could find—since for some reason, the room I was in had the heat jacked way up—and went in search of coffee.

Instead, I found Benjamin, toddling as fast as he could down the hallway toward me, eyes bright with mischief, and jaw working as he swallowed something. He was wearing a fuzzy onesie that made him look like a tiny koala bear, and had red dye smeared all around his mouth. In each fist, he had a wet candy cane tightly clutched.

I heard a yelled, "Where did he go?" and stepped in front of him.

"I think your mommy is calling, little Ben."

He stopped, almost toppling over, and a huge, almost toothless smile creased his pink-smeared face. "Can Cay, Can Cay!" He held up the candy, and I scooped him into my arms.

"That's me, Candy Kane," I agreed, carrying him back towards the shouting woman.

"Oh, thank goodness," a ponytailed, petite woman sighed as I entered the room. She was dressed in a fuzzy onesie that matched Benjamin's. "Candy! Oh my gosh, aren't you freezing?"

"Can Cay!" Benjamin crowed.

"Hi, Ben!" I tickled him under his sticky chin. "No, I'm plenty warm. You're Lindyann, right?"

"I am. And you are my favorite person in the world. Thank you for taking care of my angel last week." Her eyes sparkled, and she rested one hand on her abdomen. "I needed that second honeymoon, and when I thought Nicky was going to call me home, I almost lost my mind. Not sure how I'll handle two more."

"Twins? I know someone who runs a betasitting agency," I teased. "I bet I can set you up with a great nanny."

"Love you so much," she replied, and grabbed Benjamin from me, dropping a kiss on my cheek, then his. She pulled me into a room behind the kitchen, which had a wall of windows overlooking the mountain. The whole world was white with snow, with small deep green and brown patches showing on the pines. It was spectacular. "I'll be back in a sec, Candy. Gotta hose down the little monster." She padded away on koala bear feet.

I had to force myself to focus on the room itself. There was an enormous table along one wall, and it looked like all the family members I'd met the evening before were there. The triplets were on their phones, though they all looked up and greeted me.

None of them seemed unhappy to see me. Maybe Valentine had been wrong. I hoped not everyone was against me marrying their eldest brother.

I had a feeling I'd find out.

Luke and Teddy were filling plates with bacon and what

smelled like fresh, homemade biscuits. My stomach growled, and I wandered closer. "Is there enough for me?"

"This plate is for you, little sister," Teddy replied. "You eat bacon? Biscuits?"

"Homemade marmalade?" Luke added, placing a cup of coffee in front of me. "Caffeine?"

Teddy frowned at him. "Omegas need water. Juice. And food. She slept through dinner."

Gah. He was so protective; it reminded me of Pax. My fiancé, who wasn't here. My eyes began to sting.

"Damnit, Teddy, you're making her cry," Luke sighed. Obviously exasperated, he poured me glasses of juice and water and brought them over while Teddy piled yet another plate with cut fruit, Greek yogurt, and granola.

"I'll explode if I eat all this," I complained. "But I'll die happy." Teddy ducked his head, that blush on his cheeks again. I stuffed an enormous bite of honeyed biscuit in my mouth.

"I'll die if I don't get out on the slopes!" A young woman with cotton candy-pink hair, a light lavender ski suit, and snow boots clomped in the door, followed by another woman, a slightly older version with dark hair and a butter-yellow snowsuit.

"Penny, you know we're waiting for... Candy! You're awake," the older one called. "Happy New Year's Eve!" She came over, beaming at me. I tried to chew my biscuit and swallow it, but ended up choking and spluttering, spraying the table and the woman with crumbs.

Well, that was one way to make an unforgettable first impression: spit all over your future in-laws.

"Quick, the Heimlich maneuver!" Penny rushed over to pull me out of my chair. "Somebody call the paramedics! Thank god I took that online class." I wriggled my way out of her grip, with the help of the other girls, who were all laughing like this wasn't unusual for their little sister.

"Sorry," the dark-haired older woman—who had to be Kati—muttered. "Penny's a very dramatic soul." She handed me my water while the others shuttled Penny away, who was already apologizing. The room was filled with noise, laughter, and the sounds of family.

"It's okay, I like it," I said truthfully once I could speak again. "I always wanted siblings."

She snorted. "Not this many, I'm guessing."

I smiled, but didn't answer. I'd been lonely growing up, but nine siblings was intimidating.

Suddenly, Kati's hand was in mine, her eyes on the high neckline that covered my mate mark. "You know, we're family now. No matter what, Candy. And I think you'll be perfect for Nicky. Just... don't give up on him yet, okay? He's a little stuck in his ways."

I swallowed hard, not quite sure what to say. "I didn't mean what I said... what you probably heard."

"Even if you did, it's okay. Just give him time to change your mind." When I nodded, she gasped. "Oh! I almost forgot. Nicky sent you this." She ran to a long countertop and brought back a sleek, white box. "New phone, new number, but if I'm not mistaken, Nicky's PA will have fixed it so your contacts are all there ..."

I grinned, opening the phone. I was a pretty typical omega when it came to loving gifts, and this phone was the top of the line. He'd even sent me a rhinestone-studded phone case in red and white stripes, to match my name.

"Cute!" I powered it on while the others went back to breakfast.

"Has anyone heard from Nicky today?" Penny asked from

the other end of the table. "I thought he was supposed to be here by now."

Suddenly, the room went quiet, all eyes on me. My new phone vibrated in my hand, and I stared down at it, trying not to freak out at the dozens of messages that were appearing. Most were from Rain, Soleil, and my parents, but a bunch were from Pax. I ignored the super long thread of voice messages, and read his last text.

It was simple and disappointing.

"He thought he could make it by today," I said, trying for chipper, but that terse, apologetic message was just making me want to cry, or kill someone, or both. "The board meeting ran until the wee hours... and he had to do something important this morning. He'll still be here tonight, but around midnight."

"What could possibly keep him away?" Teddy demanded.

I shrugged. "He didn't say. Maybe he's going to surprise us somehow?"

Penny mumbled, "He already surprised me by being a douche. I'm gonna kick his butt."

"I'll text him again and see if he has a better ETA." I tapped out a quick note. "I'm sure he'll get back to me soon," I murmured, pressing a hand to my abdomen. Suddenly, the few bites of food I'd eaten felt like lead in my gut.

No one spoke for a long moment, then the room exploded into sounds and motion. "Well, midnight will be here before you know it. I think it's time to start the New Year's decorations," Kati announced. Everyone else moaned, and the triplets and Penny ran for the door. "Get back here!"

Teddy and Luke were already backing away. "We have to make sure the snowplow is scheduled... and bring in wood... and things," Luke said, panic in his eyes. *Sorry,* he mouthed silently as he and Teddy both went for the door at the same time.

I had no idea what had just happened, but a few hours later, I was contemplating faking my own death. Though Kati might actually kill me first.

We were moving pictures around in the main hallways, making space for a new one that was coming in a few days, when I finally hit my limit. I'd done Crossfit at my local gym a few times, but nothing had prepared me for hours of redecorating. We'd shifted furniture, changed sofa cushions around, placed bowls of cinnamon-scented pinecones here and there—which almost triggered my cinnamon challenge PTSD—and then she'd decide to tackle "the real work." So I'd switched to climbing ladders, holding up framed pictures, moving them one centimeter to the left, then back to the right, then up, then down.

"Kati. I can't feel my fingers. I'm going to pass out."

"That's perfect." I peered down to see Kati was now slumped on the sofa, clearly exhausted. "We have to... take a break." She had her eyes closed. "Too tired to keep on..." In a second, she was snoring, and I crept down the ladder.

Masculine laughter sounded from the doorway. For a moment, my heart leaped, thinking it was Pax. But when I whirled to face him— "Oh. Hi, Luke."

"I can't believe you outlasted Captain Kati," Luke said with a low whistle. "Would you like a drink? Or to freshen up before lunch? Have you heard from Nicky yet today?"

I forced a smile in return. "I have dozens of texts and voice messages, but haven't had time to go through them."

"Maybe you could take a moment now?" Luke's eyes were pleading. "I'm not saying you should forgive him. But maybe there's something in there that might help you feel better?"

He could tell how bad I felt? I didn't trust my voice, just nodded, and curled up in a nearby armchair to read.

It did make me feel better, at least a little. Pax had shared all sorts of funny memes, which actually had me laughing, and stories about his family's skiing trips from previous years. He'd also shared a lot of what was happening at work, which made me feel both better and worse. I knew how deeply affected he'd been by his mother's death, and I knew he'd turned his life into a quest to keep other omegas from dying like she had.

But why wouldn't he have told me at the beginning what was going on? I would have understood the importance of it. Had he thought I wouldn't care? Or maybe that I wasn't interested?

I lowered my phone, stunned. I'd asked what was going on, but I hadn't pressed. Maybe I had been part of the problem, not showing enough interest. I hadn't wanted to intrude on his home office when he'd told me he was working. My own insecurities had made me feel like I would be bothering him. Of *course* he hadn't asked me to listen to his worries and fears. He'd never had a mate around who cared.

From what I could tell, he didn't have anyone to talk to, besides his siblings. I scrolled to the last few texts, my heart lighter, just as Luke wandered back into the room with hot chocolates. "He said there's weather issues at the airport, and it's delaying him. And that he's bringing a surprise, though he hasn't told me what it is. I think he feels guilty."

Or had felt that way. His texts had ended abruptly the night before.

"Airport? Since when does he fly out of an airport? He spent millions on that damned landing strip..." Luke grumbled, pulling out his phone. "There's no bad weather anywhere from here to Atlanta, just a little band of storms moving through Texas later tonight and tomorrow. If I didn't know better, I'd say he's avoiding..."

"Me?"

He looked up at my whispered question, and froze. "Um. Maybe I'm wrong. Oh, yeah, there's a storm. Totally missed it."

Damnit. He was worse at lying than I was.

He tucked his phone away in a pocket. "Whatever it is, he owes you an apology. Make him beg on his knees, okay?"

I scratched at my neck, my mark burning. My scent rose up slightly at the thought of Pax on his knees, but the strawberries and cream smelled scorched, like a pie left too long in the oven. "Will do, Luke. Anyway, I guess he won't be here for dinner after all. Tell Kati when she wakes up that you all might need to postpone your family picture."

"Candy," he began, stepping toward me. "I'll talk to him about this. After all of the kids grew up, until you walked into his life, work was all he had to fill his time. I'm so—"

I held up a hand. Pity right now, or sympathy, would break me. "I need to rest. Kati wore me out, too."

I hid in my bathtub nest through lunchtime, knowing I probably wasn't making a good impression on Pax's family but not able to care. They'd already seen my drunken ass screeching at their brother that she didn't want him—and seen my actual ass hanging out of my dress—and if they didn't hate me from that, I figured missing lunch wasn't that big of a deal.

I had the feeling I was running a fever, so I took a few pain relievers, and turned the fan on high. Maybe I had altitude sickness? I read for a while, texted Soleil, who was still on vacation, and avoided texting Rain.

I had a feeling if I did, I'd only send one word: grapefruit.

When I called Pax, it went directly to voicemail. My texts stayed on read for another hour. Finally, my phone buzzed.

> Pax: Sorry, love. Shitstorm of the century
> followed by weather delays. Real storm
> should clear up soon. I'm trying to get there, I
> promise.

I opened my weather app. Like Luke had said, there was no weather anywhere from here to home. What was he hiding?

> Where are you? Freaking out a little. Feeling...

I thought about telling him I felt sick, but then reconsidered. He would probably call Mountain Rescue to fly me in a helicopter to the hospital.

> Feeling sad. Where are you?

> Pax: On my way to you eventually, princess. I promise it will all be okay. Go have some fun with my sisters.

For some reason, the word princess sounded condescending in my mind for the first time. *Have some fun?* My gut churned. He'd sent me to meet his entire enormous family, all alone. And even if I'd loved them instantly, that didn't make it better.

I was going to kick his *ass.*

And have some fun.

Suddenly, all the energy I'd thought was gone earlier was back.

I was in the mountains. I could ski, though not very well. I was a greens and blues girl, or at least I had been before I'd revealed as an omega, before my parents had decided skiing was too dangerous. Right now, I had access to a private lift and some of the best snow in a century.

Fuck moping. I was going to hit the slopes. Maybe today would be my black diamond debut.

I turned my phone off, stuck it in a drawer, and opened the closet. In a half hour, I was wandering through the empty lodge. Kati was still snoring on the sofa. No one else was around, though I looked. So I tucked a note about where I'd gone under her pillow, then left to burn off some of my bad mood.

Chapter 19

Pax

I'd fucked up, big time. I texted Candy again, but got no response. She'd stopped reading my texts earlier that afternoon, and my calls were going straight to voice mail. She didn't want to talk to me, and I didn't blame her.

She didn't know what had happened to keep me from making it to Colorado. No one did, not really.

Not that it should have mattered. I'd had more than one person over the years, both in and out of the family, accuse me of being a workaholic. But besides my family, my company had been everything to me.

Up until now.

I felt like a fool. By not taking the time to explain exactly what was going on, by acting like my life hadn't changed utterly the moment she'd stumbled in my front door, I'd hurt the woman I'd sworn to love forever.

I slipped my phone in my pocket, sighing at Teddy's last text, letting me know Candy was finally okay. Or at least, she'd gone skiing.

I'd shared the details about the problems at Paxson Pharma

with my siblings since they all had a major stake in the company as well. But after Victoria had sent me a sweetly worded death threat, telling me she suspected my fiancée didn't know what was going on, I realized I had never really spoken to her about it. Or even spoken to her at all, since Christmas.

I didn't even know some of the small things about her, the sort any casual boyfriend would. Sven, the flight attendant who'd accompanied her to Telluride had sent a very polite text making sure I knew she'd had a slight allergic reaction to the flowers my PA had delivered to the plane. He'd reassured me that she was fine, but seemed concerned that I hadn't been aware of her allergy.

Texts had been bubbling up every few minutes for the past two days from my sisters, who all had plans to murder me in my sleep, or skin me alive for sending Candy on alone.

I'd called Valentine to check on Candy. Valentine had always been the most soft-hearted of my sisters. But she had said, almost without any of her usual stutter, "She's f-fine, no thanks to you. I'm ashamed of you, Nicky."

And then she'd hung up.

At least Candy wasn't sitting around the lodge, moping, or coming up with ways to kill me, or break up with me. And as soon as I had Victor on my plane, I would be by her side.

And I wouldn't leave it again. Not for anything.

I thought about telling Teddy or Kati what had sent me to Dallas airport, waiting for a private jet to arrive from Santiago. But I couldn't tell my siblings about Victor yet. I didn't want to get their hopes up again... and I wasn't certain who would be stepping off that plane.

Would it be my oldest brother, who'd helped me raise our younger sisters, and been my co-CEO at Paxson Pharma until a year before?

Or would it be some broken version of him?

Or a stranger?

Victor's shout, from the opened door of the plane, had me squinting against the cold wind that blew from the deep gray clouds on the horizon. "What the fuck are you doing here, Nicky? You're supposed to be in Telluride with your woman."

My heart leaped. He sounded like his old self.

I shouted back, "You asshole, I should be. But the PI I've had tracking you all over the fucking world called me and told me you were returning to America."

"You weren't supposed to know I was coming. I was planning to surprise you. Valentine knew I was coming."

I paused. "Valentine?"

"Yes. She's the one who ordered me back before New Year's, to meet your omega."

Valentine had known where he was all along? How to reach him? I wanted to wring her neck. I'd poured hundreds of thousands of dollars into tracking him down.

Victor started down the airstair, and I managed a grin. What was done was done.

My brother looked like a shell of his former self. If I hadn't known it was his flight, I might not have recognized him. His dark hair was the same, but the beard from the photo had filled out, and the lines of strain around his eyes were far more pronounced than they had been when he left the US. But they eased when he looked down at what he was holding.

Holy shit.

At the *baby* he was holding.

"Victor?" I managed to say as he turned and handed the baby to the elderly woman who'd followed him down the steps. The flight attendant carried out a car seat and handed it to my brother. Finally, I remembered how to speak. "How... Whose?"

Victor smiled down at the infant, peeling back a corner of the blanket swaddling it, and showed me. "This is Señora

Vazquez, my newest employee. And this is Paloma, my daughter."

A thousand questions filled my mind. Only one came out. "How?"

His smile vanished. "I needed a reason to live. I found one." I could tell I wasn't getting any more, so I accepted it and escorted them back to my car. My plane was waiting on the other side of the corporate aviation terminal, and it should have been a matter of minutes to be on board and flying to Telluride.

But lightning struck two miles from the airport before we could make it to my plane. The airport staff sent us back into the terminal, to the executive lounge, to wait. While I paced, Victor sent lounge staff to buy enough infant supplies and formula for the baby, and got the older woman and the baby settled in a private room with a bed and a small crib. The lightning stopped an hour later.

And then, in true Dallas fashion, the hail began. Chunks of ice the size of baseballs pelted the tarmac outside the viewing windows.

My phone battery had died, and I plugged it in to charge, while Victor picked out the healthiest options on the menu for us both. I ordered a glass of Balvenie, though Victor declined, and told a succinct version of his travels over the past year, and the story of how he came to be a father.

"So you adopted her at her mother's request?" I asked, rolling up my sleeve and scratching at my mate mark. "I'm sorry Paloma lost her mother. But you'll be a fantastic dad. Will you want to move back into the house while she's young, or...?" I scratched harder, wincing when I inadvertently drew blood.

Victor's eyes narrowed, and he changed the subject. "How long ago did you say you claimed your omega?"

"Five days—no, six, now," I replied, trying not to claw at my arm. "But I need to see a doctor. Something's wrong with my mark."

"What does it feel like?"

"Like a rash? No. Like it's... burning. Like I've burned myself."

He swore. "Your mate had the mini-heat, yes? When you met."

I blinked. "Yes, but I didn't mark her then. I waited until later." I blushed. "I mean, a few days later."

He ran a hand over his face. "That's not a rash, brother. That's a biological imperative you're feeling. Your mate is going into heat."

"That's impossible. She told me she's not due for her heat for nine or ten more months... Oh *shit*." I dropped my tumbler of whiskey on the plush carpet. "The annual shot. Could she have been..." I strode to a nearby table where a courtesy laptop was open, ignoring both Victor and the employee who came to clean up my spill, and called my PA.

"Mr. Paxson?" he answered, groggy from sleep.

"Theodore, wake up. I need you to check the records on which doctors and clinics in the Georgetown area, if any, may have received the mislabeled shots. Text me the list *immediately*." The main shipments had gone to New York and New Jersey, but if one of the doctors had a satellite office in either of those states, and part of their order had been transferred to a Georgetown branch...

I hung up before he could speak. By the time he called back, I'd logged into my Storm Security account and pulled up the dossier I'd had done on Candy the first day we'd met. When he listed the names of the doctors' offices who were involved, I cursed out loud.

"Dr. Marguerite Grantham. Fuck. *Fuck!*"

"What is it, Nicky?" Victor murmured.

"You're right." I explained about the shots, and he took it in as he always had. Calmly, efficiently calculating the best steps forward.

I'd sent my new mate off to Colorado, alone, going into her annual heat.

"How did you know?" I rasped, holding my burning mate mark with one hand. "No one's ever mentioned any side effects like this."

"Normally, once the mating bites are exchanged, both partners are out of danger. But it's highly unusual for true mates to be apart for more than a day or two, and never for an annual heat. We have to get you to your omega as fast as possible, Nicky."

"She's suffering, I know. God, it's my fault. I should've gone with her. No, I should have *waited* to claim her. I'm so fucking selfish."

He didn't disagree. "I hope the weather clears and you get there in time." Something in his tone had me wrenching my head up.

"What do you mean?"

"I'm sure our family will help her. I can't see Lin, or any of the omegas who know what's happening... Well, they'll have seen the signs. They'll get her to a doctor."

"What?"

His eyes flashed with anger and frustration. "This is her first mated heat, Nick. She'll be going into it without you. Without you there, her fever could rise higher and higher, until she slips into a coma. She could suffer permanent brain damage."

"No!" I was up and halfway out the door to the lounge before he caught me. "Let me go. I'm taking a car."

"You can't drive in the storm," he said quietly, fighting to hold me. "And it's a fifteen-hour drive to get to what could be snowed-in passes. Plane is the fastest way to get to her. Be patient." He held out my phone, which had charged up enough to work. "Let the girls know."

Of course. I powered it on, and saw a barrage of texts had come in on the emergency family chat.

No one could find Candy. They hadn't seen her for hours, but she'd left a note Teddy had found saying she was going skiing. But she was still gone, the lifts had stopped, and it was getting dark with no sign of her.

They promised to find her for me and get her medical assistance if she needed it.

My fingers trembled as I typed the messages to let them know that she already needed medical help. When the phone rang, I spoke to Kati, who was the calmest of us all in a crisis. She tried to keep the censure out of her tone, but it was there.

And I deserved it.

Victor picked up the phone when I dropped it, and spoke with Kati for a long while before hanging up. Finally, he said, "They'll get her help, Nicky. Don't worry. You know we've got your back, just like you always had ours."

Agony raced through my arm, and my heart. "I should never have left her side. The thought of her hurting, suffering, when I'm so far away... God, if I could go back and do it again —" I stopped when Victor let out a sigh.

"What are you planning to change, Nicky?"

"What do you mean?" I frowned. "I'm sure as hell never going to leave her side."

"How are you going to make that happen? I haven't been here for a while, but before I left, all you did was work. It was your reason to get up in the mornings, and what you thought about every hour of every day. Are you going to let that go?" His shadowed eyes were filled with compassion. "She's your reason, isn't she?"

I nodded, dumbly.

"So what are you going to do differently from this moment on?"

"I'm done." I stood, pacing back and forth. I knew exactly what I had to do. "I'm done with *all* of it. Unless it's helping her reach her dreams. Unless I'm at her side, none of it fucking matters."

"That's the right answer, brother. I'll help you however I can. And I promise, when you get there, it'll be okay."

My laugh was hollow and humorless. "It'll never be okay. She'll never forgive me. She *should* never forgive me. I promised to be there, promised her mother I'd put her daughter first, and I didn't even make it three days before I deserted her. I'm not worthy of my omega."

"None of us are worthy, brother," Victor said quietly. "All we can do is try not to let them realize it. And never stop trying to be better, for them."

His eyes closed as he murmured, "For her."

Chapter 20

Candy

I was as sick as I'd ever been. I still thought it might be altitude sickness, but it was every bit as bad as the flu. All I knew was that I wasn't well, and that I had a fever. I wasn't thinking clearly enough to understand what was really happening.

The last thing I remembered was falling into a snowbank, and not accidentally.

I'd gotten onto a run that was far too advanced, so I'd taken off my skis and was side stepping through a wooded area, on my way to the next lift. I knew I was acting irrationally—I should've flagged down one of the skiers racing past, but they looked large, like alphas, and I couldn't stand the idea of any of them close to me.

The only alpha I wanted was Pax. I was so tired. Tired of waiting for him to arrive, tired of feeling like I was the only one of us who wanted to be together. Tired of feeling like I wasn't enough for him, that he'd never love me.

Or be around me long enough to even fall in love.

He would probably marry me out of some sense of obligation, though. He was so responsible, always thinking of others... and I was selfish for wanting to be the one who he thought of first. Most often.

But even if it wasn't fair, even if it was immature of me to need it, I wanted to come first for Pax. I wanted to be his focus, not his distraction.

My mate mark flared up like a fresh burn on my neck. Our biology had more or less forced us to claim each other. But it couldn't force us to stay together.

That was obvious. It was New Year's, and I was alone. He'd lied about his flight, the weather, maybe even lied about wanting to marry me. He'd never talked about love. Maybe he'd never love me.

He was probably with Dr. Murray right now, telling her how much he respected her. How pretty and perfect and professional she was...

I should take off my ring, I decided. *If I'm not going to be his wife, I shouldn't pretend.*

I pulled a glove off, but when I stared down, it was the wrong one. My right hand. So I grabbed the other one and finally got the ring off. I wanted to throw it as far as I could away from me, but my arms were as weak as well as hot. So I let the ring fall to the ground instead, then buried both hands into the snow, sighing in relief. The cold of the snow felt so good on my hot skin.

I was so hot, everywhere. Maybe I needed more snow. I ripped at my ski clothing, unable to get anything but my gloves and hat off in the end. That would have to be enough. Finally, I scooted over to a deep drift of snow and buried myself in it as deeply as I could.

Then I closed my eyes.

I dreamed of being on a rocket ship, going toward the sun. It kept getting hotter and hotter, and the astronaut next to me kept snarling that I was useless in space... and then we weren't in space. We were on a beach, and I was burning on the hot sand, while Pax swam and played in the surf with tall, blonde, wealthy omegas who had perfect teeth and perky tits.

None of them had swimsuits on, and they all had perfect Brazilian wax jobs and PhDs in aerospace engineering.

"I'll cut a bitch," I heard a woman say in my dream. Or was it a dream? "And by bitch, I mean my stupid fucking brother." It wasn't Rain, though it sounded like her. "Where did they find her?"

"In a snowbank. She was trying to cool off." A masculine voice, but not the one I wanted. I snarled, warning him away.

"F-frostbite?" This woman sounded like she was crying. "Her f-fingers."

"No, they'll be fine. Her heat kept all her extremities safe, even after an hour... The ring's gone, though."

"Mom's ring?"

"We'll send crews to search for it... metal detectors..." The voice faded.

I wasn't sure what was happening, but I heard yelling. Then someone was there, a woman, placing pills on my tongue and holding a glass of water up to my lips. I was parched, and I drank greedily, whimpering when the water was withdrawn.

"It's okay, little sister."

Sister? I didn't have any sisters. Only he did, and they wouldn't be mine now. I fought a sob. I'd wanted sisters. I'd wanted him. But he hadn't wanted me. He'd left me after he promised to take care of me. Hadn't come back when he'd said.

Hadn't loved me.

166

"Not sister," I gasped, clawing at my neck, which had flared up like someone had pressed a brand to it. "Ahh!"

"Candy, you're going to be fine. Just wait a few minutes. I gave you some temporary heat suppressants since Nicky isn't here."

Someone else cursed. "Those work for a day or two, tops. Where the fuck *is* he?"

I whined and raised a hand to my neck after she placed something there, over my mating bite. A cloth? I tried to tear it away, but hands held mine down.

"No, sweetness, you're bleeding already. Don't scratch. These pills will help, and Nicky—"

"Pax," I managed to say. "Pax is here?" Why did that worry me? Was he coming to tell me I wasn't good enough, old enough, smart enough... I fought to open my eyes.

"S-soon. Just sleep." I felt a small body, a woman, slip in beside mine, then felt a vibration against my back. Someone was purring, of all things.

She smelled vaguely of cinnamon and vanilla, and I fell back to sleep in her arms.

Chapter 21

Candy

"Are you awake?"

"Stop yelling," I moaned, then wondered why I was yelling. I blinked. It was dark. The world felt hazy and odd. And someone who smelled like cinnamon and vanilla was touching me.

My stomach lurched, like I might be sick. The sensation of whoever's skin it was made me want to peel off my own.

"Please," I begged. "Please don't touch."

"Of c-course."

I opened my eyes and saw the outline of a young woman. She was sitting on the edge of a bed. Not the guest bed, not the room they'd given me with my bathtub nest close by. This bed was bigger, and smelled like... "Pax?" I was in his room, but he wasn't here, of course. It was just me and one of his sisters. I smelled cinnamon and pine. "Valentine? Why am I... How did I get here?"

She whispered the answer, her stutter almost gone. "You fell into a snowbank, off-piste on a black run. No one knew you'd g-gone out. By the time Luke found your note, all the lifts

168

had stopped running. Ski patrol..." She paused. "You went into heat; that's all that saved you."

I sucked in a breath as a shaft of light illuminated the room. "That's not possible. I had a mating heat with Pax already, and I'm on the annual shot. I can't have a heat until—"

"Apparently, you can," another woman said from the doorway. It was Lin, holding a tray with a steaming pot of tea, a pile of shortbread, and some crackers and cheese. She looked like she'd been crying. "We've been texting and calling Nicky the whole time, since we found you. He feels terrible that he's not here. Worse than terrible."

"But he's... not here?"

"He's on his way. I swear."

I held up a hand. I didn't know if I wanted to hear his excuses. I wasn't sure I wanted to even see him. "Can I have my phone, please?"

She passed it to me. I opened it. Soleil was still in the Caribbean somewhere, but Rain? She'd show up with a shovel, duct tape, and no questions asked.

I typed in two words.

> Pig farm.

> Rain: FUCK. Grapefruit???

> Not yet. Maybe. TTYS.

> Rain: Pigs it is. On my way.

Lin sat on the edge of the bed while Valentine slipped away. "He had reasons, believe it or not, Candy. Not all of them were good, but Nicky needs to be the one to tell you everything that happened."

"No, he doesn't. He may not have said it aloud, but he's

made it clear over the past week that he doesn't see me as... Well." I had to close my mouth, or I'd scream. Or cry. Finally, I squeaked out, "I wasn't his priority, was I? I don't know that I ever will be."

"Don't say that. Please, give him another chance. This was all just a series of awful timing, bad weather, and misunderstandings. He loves you, I swear—"

"I don't want to talk about Pax."

She chewed at her lip. "Then can I at least tell you why you went into heat?" When I nodded, she went on. "The Paxson Pharma shot we all take, the annual one? You know there was a mislabeling at one of the factories. We thought it was all doses that went to the Northeast, but a few doctors in other states got some of the bad batches."

"Dr. Grantham?"

She nodded. "She's Valentine's doctor, too, so Kati has been freaking out. There are way too many hot alpha ski bums here." I closed my eyes as she went on. "My brother had no idea you could possibly go into your heat when he put you on the plane. He didn't know your doctor was one of the affected ones. He called a dozen times in the night to check on you."

"He didn't come." It was all I could say. "He promised. And he lied about the weather."

"No, actually, there was a weather delay, but he was in Dallas. He found out on his way here that our brother Victor was coming home. When I tell you about Victor, you'll understand."

I held up a shaking hand, and noticed it was bare. I had no idea where the ring Pax had given me was, not that it mattered now. "If he wanted me to know, he would have told me. I get it. I'm not family."

Her eyes went wide. "But you *are*. You're everything to him."

I blinked at her, my head still aching, and wondered if it would be rude to ask her to leave. "Obviously not. I want to go home." I tried to swing my legs out of the bed, but she held my arm.

"You can't. He'll be here with Victor any minute now. Here, have some tea."

I pretended to settle down, but I used the moment when she stirred honey in the tea to pick up my phone and text Rain one more time, with only one word.

Grapefruit.

Lin kept talking, nervously and quickly. "It's not safe for you to go; the doctor said your heat is only suppressed. And I promise Pax will explain it all better. He thinks you'll never forgive him for this whole mess—that you won't want to stay with him." She wiped her streaming eyes.

"She *shouldn't* stay with me."

The voice at the door was the one I'd wanted most in the world to hear for the past few days. But his words cut me to my core.

"Nicky, you idiot! Finally." Lin stood, leaving the tea, and punched him hard on the arm as she passed. Then she gave him a hug, whispering something in his ear before they both turned their heads toward me. I closed my eyes, trying not to let her, or him, see how his words had devastated me. "Every time I think you couldn't fuck this up worse, you do. Explain what you meant," she ordered before she slipped out of the room.

"What–what I meant?" he sputtered, then gasped as I began to throw my feet over the edge of the bed, though each leg weighed a thousand pounds and standing made me dizzy.

"I heard you, Pax. Don't worry. I won't stay."

Rain was on her way. She'd take me somewhere I could recover. She'd survived losing her true mate. I would, too.

Before I knew what was happening, Pax had stormed across the room, and had me in his arms. "Oh, fuck. No, Candy, sweetheart, no!"

I tried to keep myself stiff while he held me steady, tried not to let him see how broken I was. But the simple touch of his skin on mine was enough to bring all the memories back of my birthday and Christmas, and before, when we were snowed in. All the wonders of discovering my true mate.

And then the agony of realizing the dream wasn't reality. And I wasn't his love at all.

I was just his mate. A trick fate had played on him.

I'd felt, for a few days, like it might work. That his life would change as radically as mine had. I wanted him at the center of it all. Whether I worked, or went to school, or whatever the future held... I'd seen him there with me, beside me. I'd wanted to build a life with him more than anything in the world.

I'd believed that the mark he'd left on my neck meant he wanted the same.

Maybe before he'd claimed me, when he'd told me I was too young, he hadn't meant I was too young to be tied to him for life.

He'd meant I wasn't enough. I wasn't worthy of being put first.

It felt like everything good in the world, all my plans for the future, had been stripped away before I'd even begun to realize them. I was teetering on the brink of collapse, so I closed my eyes before he could see what he'd done to me.

"Let me go," I begged. "Just let me go."

"Wherever you go, I will go. I will never leave you again. I promise."

"Your promises don't mean anything."

"Tell me," he whispered.

So I did. I opened my mouth and all of it came pouring out, all of the fear and worry and hurt. The pain of knowing I would never be his priority. How I didn't measure up to his perfect doctor colleague. How he had hurt me by not telling the world we were together. By not telling anyone, besides his siblings.

He stood still, holding me, taking it. Listening, until at last I fell silent, and opened my eyes again, really looking at him for the first time.

His skin was paler than it had ever been, his hair mussed, as if he'd run his hands through it a thousand times. His lips and jaw were tight, suppressing emotions, but his eyes...

"Pax?" I croaked. Tears leaked from his bloodshot eyes as he stared at me like... like I was precious to him. Like all my dreams had been real.

But there was agony behind the softness. A knife turned inward, and I could feel its sharp edge in the mate bond with him this close. It was like he hated himself for hurting me.

"You said I shouldn't stay," I mumbled, confused.

"When I said that, I meant you should hate me. You should never want to see me again, for letting you get hurt. For sending you away alone, not putting you first." He stroked a hand down the side of my face, agony in every word. "I don't deserve you. I never did. But I'm going to try and convince you to give me another chance. To show you that you're all that I care about from now on."

I shook my head. It sounded good, but I knew as soon as this was over, he'd be back to running his company. Shutting me out. Treating me like a child.

"No, Pax. You were right. I'm not old enough or accomplished enough for the CEO of Paxson Pharma." I tried to picture myself sitting at his side at a shareholder meeting, or standing beside him at a press conference.

People would think I was his intern. Or worse, like Dr. Murray. His teenaged sister.

I'd seen his embarrassment.

"You already raised your siblings. You don't want to raise a dumb omega who doesn't even understand what your job requires," I tried to joke, though my voice was hoarse. "I'll go back to college, or something. Maybe start a pig farm."

His jaw trembled. "Then we'll be pig farmers together. I need a new job. I resigned my position as CEO of Paxson an hour ago."

"What?" A strange tingling raced along my limbs, like they'd been asleep and were waking back up. "You can't do that!"

He shrugged. "I can. I already did."

"But... the shots that went wrong. Your sister said that you had to oversee the fallout and—"

He pressed a soft finger on my lips. "I knew I'd fucked up letting you leave the day you walked out of my office. I compounded my error when I gave you the choice to go back to your parents' house. Your home isn't there anymore." He pressed a hand to his heart. "It's here. And my home..." He swallowed. "I won't have one without you in it."

I didn't know what to think. "You lied to me, though. About the weather?"

"No. I was on my way to the airport when an email came in from my private investigator. My brother, Victor—the one no one could find—was on his way back from South America. He's home for good. With my brothers and sisters helping, Victor's going to take over the business, the response to the shots, all of it. I informed the board on the flight, and he's stepping up, effective immediately. I'm going to do what I've always wanted to do."

"What is that?" I asked, deeply curious, though my stomach was beginning to cramp in a way that I recognized.

He set me down on the bed and kneeled over me, still stroking my hair back. "I'm going to be selfish for a change."

"What do you mean?"

"I've spent my life taking care of my siblings and my company. Putting them first, and not what I needed." His other hand moved to my breast, cupping it gently. "I'm going to be selfish, and love you and *only* you, from now until you forgive me. Even if it takes the rest of our lives."

I ignored the word love. I wasn't sure what he meant by it. My mate mark still burned, and my heart was still bruised. But I set that conversation aside, losing myself in the feel of his strong hands on me. For a while, he massaged me gently. Whispering words of apology and promises that I would never be alone again, he soothed me enough that my hands dropped to the bedding, and I began stroking the cloth beneath us, moving it into place.

Unconsciously, I arched my back, pressing my breast into his grip and shivering as his fingers found my nipple through the sheer fabric of my nightgown, tightening around it. His nostrils flared as a rush of my scent filled the air.

"Selfish, you said? I don't think I want a selfish lover," I whispered as my core cramped again, sending more slick into my soaked panties.

"Then I'll need to convince you, Omega. Because I'm greedy, too. For the feel and the taste of you. The sight of your curves."

He undid the ribbon at the neck of the nightgown, then grunted as he noticed the line of tiny buttons on the front. "I think it's your sister's—" I began, but he'd already taken it in both hands and ripped it down the middle.

"What if what I need to soothe my guilt is to suck these tits, and lick your sweet cunt until you can't remember what it feels like not to be shaking with pleasure?"

"Is... Is that what you need?" I managed to ask as his mouth moved to my breasts, sucking and pulling at my nipples, starting up a spiral of need in my center. "You only want to... please me?"

"Yes, princess. That's all I want, and all I'll ever do, from this day on. In bed and out."

I knew better than to let my body take over. We still needed to talk. But my body chose that moment to remember what I was.

I was an omega in heat. And the time for words was over.

Chapter 22

Pax

In one moment, I was kissing my beloved's perfect pink nipples.

In the next, she was growling, snarling at me, and had flipped us over, her hands yanking at the buttons on my shirt and my belt. Her deep brown eyes flashed with a strange fire, her face was flushed and red, and her fingers were hot on my own warm skin.

The mating heat she'd endured had been nowhere near this intense, and I knew this was only the beginning. Annual heat cycles only ended after a week... or a bit earlier if the omega became pregnant. Of course, omegas who had found their mate could become pregnant even outside their heat cycles, but the probability rose exponentially during a heat.

Candy was fertile right now.

My heart raced at the thought of her swollen with my child, *our* child. But it wasn't pounding only out of fear—though I would never lose my belief that pregnancy was dangerous, no matter how good the doctors, how effective the medicines.

There was also excitement at the thought of starting a new family, one of our own. We might have a dark-haired girl like her, with her optimism and open heart. Or a boy, with her compassion and humor. Or one of each.

If she wanted it, I would keep her pregnant for years, watching her breasts swell and fill with milk, her body grow rounder, softer. She would be the best mother alive.

A dark, almost primal need to stuff her full of my seed, to keep her begging for more consumed my thoughts. I wanted to stuff her to overflowing, fill her again and again.

Breed her.

She whined in frustration at my clothing. "Hush, Omega. Let me take them off."

"Too slow," she growled, her mouth descending to my chest as soon as I had it uncovered. To my shock, she bit me hard enough to break the skin, then lapped at the small wound, like an animal.

Fuck. It hurt, but my cock didn't seem to get that message. Seeing the smeared blood on her lips as she left hickeys everywhere she kissed—as if she were marking her territory, claiming me dozens of times—was one of the hottest things I'd ever seen. My erection was so painful, I wondered if I'd sprained something inside.

Candy kept biting and licking at me, more gently now, as I shucked off my clothing and pulled the sheets back. She halted me with another growl. "No!" There was a sharpness in her tone I'd never heard. "*My* nest."

"Okay, sweetheart." I moved as if to step out of it, but her shriek stopped me.

"In the middle," she ordered, pointing imperiously at the center of the king-sized mattress.

I had never heard of this. Usually, omegas built their nests, then invited the alpha in. But as she began moving around me, I realized she wasn't taking any chances that I might disappear again, or not come back in.

She was building her nest around me, and as I watched, it dawned on me that this was just how I planned to build my life.

Around her. Her in the center. Her at the core of *every* decision I made, every step I took, every breath I inhaled. She was mine, yes. But I was also hers—body, mind, and soul.

"Omega, if you want me to stay in your nest, I will," I crooned, purring as she fussed with blankets and pillows. "I will stay in it for the rest of our lives."

"Yes," she hissed, those eyes snapping fire again. "Now, knot."

I grinned. It was far too soon to knot her; it would take a few orgasms before she was softened enough to accept even my full length. But I nodded. "Sit on me, Omega. Sit here, and let me taste your slick. I'm so thirsty."

"Hmmm," she replied, purring herself now, though her cheeks were rosy. She maneuvered herself to sit over me, her hands on the walnut headboard, then lowered her pussy directly over my face. I grasped her upper thighs in both hands and dove in.

I devoured her, burying my face in her sweet center. No matter how many times I licked her, tasted her, felt her shuddering in my grasp, it was not enough. It would *never* be enough. I wanted to imprint my tongue on her clit, kiss and nibble and lick at her so thoroughly she would feel my touch when she was awake, or asleep. She was more than a woman— she was my soul's other half, and I tried to tell her that with every touch, every swirl of my tongue on her hot skin.

I felt her coming again and again as I held her down over

my face. I didn't need air. I didn't need space. All I needed was her clit, her honey-soaked cunt, and her cries of pleasure.

I fucked her with my tongue as deeply as I could, lapping every droplet of her juices I could reach. Then I licked down to the rosebud of her ass, loving the way she protested weakly, before allowing the intimacy of my tongue in her tight back passage.

I wanted to fuck her there as well, stretch her slowly, then fill every one of her holes with my cum. But not now. Not until I'd pumped her pussy full of my seed, and a baby was growing inside her.

"Pax!" she shouted as she came for what had to be the tenth time, before I pulled away.

"Yes, my sweet girl. What do you need?"

"Your knot," she murmured, her speech slurred. Her skin was overly hot, and I knew she truly did need it. It was time.

I moved her down so that her drenched entrance was at the tip of my thick cock, and smiled up into her flushed face. "It's yours, sweetness. Fuck yourself down onto me."

My eyes stung with tears at the beauty of her. How had I ever been so fortunate to have her walk into my life, saving me from the slog my days had become? Before Candy, my life had been a series of chores. But like the fool I'd never thought I was, I'd almost stayed with my routine, prioritizing the less important things in my life over her.

I'd come so close to losing her.

"Forgive me, my love," I rasped, as she finally managed to work my last inch inside, her walls clenched tightly around me. She was panting with the exertion of opening herself around my thick cock. "Forgive me for being an idiot. For not being the alpha you needed, or deserved."

She panted her reply, her gaze clearing slightly as she gave me a trembling smile. "Don't you... remember? Forgiveness is free. All you have to do... is ask for it."

"I will ask, and then show you." She gasped as I began to thrust up into her, the slick covering her and my cock making the first swell of my knot slip inside her. She clenched around me, then relaxed, sliding down, her perfect pussy opening to allow my entrance, until her hips met mine, and my knot held us together.

A knot wasn't sufficient to hold our hearts in place, though. As I rutted her, I planned how I would seduce her heart as well as her body.

No matter how long it took, or how hard she made me work for it.

After that first time, we rested for a while. She fell asleep with my knot still inside her, and when she woke, it seemed as if the suppressants had worn off completely. Her heat arrived like a hurricane of passion, as she became insatiable.

Every few hours, a soft knock on the door indicated the arrival of food, cold juice, and water. Each time I slipped away from the nest, Candy growled until I returned, then staked her claim once more. My skin was littered with pink bite marks, and I never wanted them to fade.

On the first day after my arrival, I was able to speak to Kati for a few moments.

"Nicky, some woman just came storming in, said she was going to cut off a grapefruit and feed it to pigs. The guards stopped her outside. Dark hair, tiny, an omega by her scent. Should we call the police?"

I winced, pulling my robe more tightly around me as I accepted her offering of pineapple juice and a charcuterie board. "No, that's Candy's best friend. Put her up in a spare room."

"I think she scared the guards," Kati whisper-shouted, as Candy began to stir behind me. "Should we really let her run loose here?"

"A room in a hotel, then. And make sure she's taken care of. Rain doesn't have money to spare."

"We called Candy's parents. Should we fly them up as well?" She wrinkled her nose. "Maybe after a few more days?"

"If they want to be here, go ahead. I'll owe you."

Her eyes shimmered with emotion. "You'll never owe any of us a damn thing, Nicky. None of us can ever repay you for all you did after Mom and Dad died. Now it's our turn to take care of you, and your omega."

I tried to fill two small words with all the love I had for my siblings. "Thank you."

Outside, I heard a woman shouting about all alphas being pigs, before her voice was muffled.

"I need you to stay if you can. Tell the rest of the family if they want to get back to work, go ahead. We'll gather at the house sometime soon."

"Are you kidding? Everyone's taking the week to get to know Paloma while Victor's holed up in the conference room, conducting online meetings. He's 'retired' half the board."

"It's his choice. I've made mine."

"Nicky? You made the right one." She quietly closed the door as Candy began whining on the bed behind me.

Two days passed, and to my surprise, Candy's heat haze began to clear. She was still feverish, and if I didn't knot her at least every few hours, she would descend into the mindless haze, but for some reason, she was more coherent than I'd expected. In between lovemaking, we began to share stories of our childhoods, and she told me about the most important people in her life: her parents and her two best friends.

I made a mental note not to be alone in a room with Rain Torres for at least a few years. I had a feeling she knew how to hold a grudge, and I'd earned her distrust.

"She'll forgive you in about a decade," Candy laughed. "She responds well to dark chocolate raspberry croissants, gift certificates to classic movie festivals, and any flavor ice cream except mint chocolate chip."

"You really know your friends." I nuzzled her hair, drawing her rich strawberries and cream scent into my lungs. "I love that." Just as it had before, that word had her tensing up. I massaged her shoulders, purring lightly, until she relaxed. "Is this what your heats are normally like? Don't get me wrong, I like being able to talk."

"They always gave me heat suppressants," she said, as I fed her some honeyed brie on a cracker. "Maybe that's part of it? What are other omegas' heats like?"

"I wouldn't know. I've knotted omegas before—" Her growl was immediate, and loud enough to shut me up. I loved hearing it, knowing what it meant. Her inner omega was possessive and protective, just like my alpha nature. "But never during a heat. Our mating heat is the only one I've ever participated in. And now, of course."

"You never..." Her voice trailed off, and the air filled with more of her scent. I could feel her lips curving up into a smile against my bare chest. "I like that. Mine. All mine, from now on."

"And you're mine, princess. Forever." I slid her up the rumpled sheets, lowered my teeth to her mating mark, and bit down gently.

That set her off, and within minutes, she was perched atop me, sliding herself down over my knot. I met her gaze, trying to tell her with my eyes all the things she wasn't ready to hear. To tell her that I might not have been in love with her when I claimed her—or at least I hadn't realized what I was feeling was the beginnings of love—but sometime in the past few days, that had changed.

When she bit her lip, tears coursing down her flushed cheeks, but her eyes shining with the same emotion, I hoped she'd understood. But I said it aloud to be sure. "I'm here, princess. I'm here from now on. It will just get bigger every time I look at you."

She blinked, then shouted with laughter. "I hope not. The damned thing's the size of a grapefruit now, Pax!"

My own laughter filled the room. "Little minx, are you laughing at my knot?"

"No one would laugh at it," she whispered, still giggling. "It's a threat all on its own." The vibrations of her laughter had her walls squeezing my knot even more tightly. "I swear, Pax, how are you still coming? I had no idea."

"I've been saving up for decades, princess. I've got a backlog."

"Backlog," she muttered. "Is that what they're calling it these days? And here I thought I'd mated an old man who wouldn't bother me with his sexual needs—"

She stopped talking when I swatted her breast lightly. "So fucking naughty." I sat up, putting my hand over her abdomen. I loved the idea of her being filled with my cum, breeding her. If it made me a pervert to want to do every last, depraved sexual act I could think of with her, so fucking be it. "My knot's the perfect size for you. You know, naughty girls get punished."

She went still, but her perfume swirled around her. "With spankings?"

"Mmmm. You liked your last one a little too much, I think. I might have to get creative." I moved my hand around to her back entrance, brushing over the tight rosebud with one slick-soaked finger. "Naughty girls get knotted everywhere."

"Promises, promises." She squirmed on my cock, and I pinched her nipple to get her to be still. "I'm not sure you've got enough energy to try, gramps."

My cock jumped, as if it knew what came next. "Princess? You're about to find out just how much energy I have."

Chapter 23

Candy

Talk *a big talk, pay a big price, Candy.*

I didn't know what I'd been thinking, challenging my alpha like that. I had no sooner finished my taunt than he had me off his knot, my pussy literally gushing with his cum and my slick, and pressed facedown to the bed again, one of his huge hands spanning the back of my neck.

"Do you trust me?" he murmured.

"I do," I said, meaning it. Sometime in the past few days, I'd learned just who my mate was. How deeply he cared, and not just about others. About me.

And I was excited to try something new.

"Hold still, baby girl. I don't want to hurt you," he growled. I relaxed. I knew whatever he did, he wouldn't hurt me. He loved me. I felt it in my heart, as certain of his affection now as I was that the sun would rise.

And I loved him. Even though I'd been convinced he didn't only days before, something had changed. Was it him quitting his job? Maybe.

It also could be the way he looked at me, like I was all he could ever see.

It also didn't hurt that he was so unbelievably sexy. Everything about him was what I would have chosen if I'd been able to design him from my own wildest dreams... and now I could feel his devotion, like a pulse of energy in my mating mark, every second.

I trusted him with my heart, and my body.

So I opened my legs slightly, letting the feeling of his smooth, velvety head rubbing the lubricating slick and cum all around my ass begin to build a new kind of pleasure inside me. I'd loved having his finger in there, but this was a lot bigger.

He pulled my hips back, one hand dropping low to toy with my clit, and began pressing at the tight ring of muscle, gently at first. Suddenly, the head slipped in, and my ass contracted around him again, tight as can be.

"God, you feel so fucking good. Open up, push back, baby. Let your alpha inside."

"Yes, sir," I breathed, then regretted it as I felt his cock swell inside me, stretching me even more. "You like that—when I call you sir."

"So much, princess." His voice was a dark promise. "Now relax." He gripped my hips and began sliding in and out, deeper with each thrust, praising me the whole time. I had wondered if it would hurt since I'd only ever played with toys back there, and the pressure was intense, but he was patient and moved inch by inch. After a few moments of the slick making his glide a smooth, wonderful torture, I relaxed entirely.

"More, *please*," I begged. "I want all of you." He surged forward, and I moaned with the intense pleasure of it.

"Oh sweetheart, you feel so incredible, I want to fuck this ass every day of my life. Wake you up in the morning and bend you over, and fill you... every... fucking... where..." He'd gotten faster, and was now plunging the full length of his cock in and out.

A dark, terrible pleasure began to build, deep inside my core. I was almost afraid of what this orgasm would feel like when it poured over me.

"Oh, my sweet omega," Pax crooned, pressing me into the mattress. "Gonna knot you now. Need you to relax even more." He set his lips next to my ear and began purring. He purred gently and fucked me roughly, until I felt boneless, then he barked, "Push back. Open up, Omega!"

His bark had my body obeying before I could process what he meant. I felt the knot push inside me, impossibly large, felt my body take over to obey him. To make room for a knot in a place that shouldn't be able to take one.

Felt his ropes of hot cum filling my tight, forbidden channel.

And his teeth in my neck again, sucking on his mate mark, turning the shock and pain into an ecstasy I'd never imagined. I came and came, feeling his knot pressing deeper into me, his hot spend overfilling my ass, until the pleasure was too much to bear, and I fell into darkness.

Three more days passed, then four, and by the end of the week, the strangely mild heat had diminished to almost nothing. But the love I felt for my mate had grown until I wasn't sure if I could keep it to myself. But he hadn't said the words, and neither had I.

"Pax? You know you were right," I murmured. He was lying behind me, his chest to my back and his knot lodged just inside my pussy, the aftershocks of our last bout of lovemaking still thrumming though my limbs.

But it was time to get up. My heat was over. Somewhere else in the lodge, I could hear Benjamin's shouts of joy, an infant's tiny cries, and Pax's family arguing and laughing.

"Yes, love? Right about what?"

"Orgasms do make the best apologies."

"Brat." He nuzzled my neck, his free hand toying lazily with my breast.

"You know what this means, right?"

"That we can never look any of my family in the face again?" he teased. "Not after you screamed for me to knot your ass until my cum poured out of your—"

Reaching back, I slapped my hand over his mouth. "They won't say a word. It's the elevator fart rule." He let out a puzzled hum, obviously confused. "Haven't you ever farted in an elevator? We are going to follow the unspoken law and pretend it never happened. They are grown-ass adults and will do the same. And if you ever bring it up, you'll never get a knot anywhere near my asshole again, you... asshole!"

We both burst out laughing, and his knot popped out of me. I giggled as he reached down and caught the liquid that was trying to spill out onto the sheets, then stuffed it gently back into my swollen channel. He'd done that a lot, almost obsessed with keeping me stuffed full of his cum.

"Pax, you know this means we could have a baby."

He leaned up on one elbow, his face strangely blank. "I know. Even with solid birth control in place, first heats that are shared by true mates very frequently result in pregnancy."

"You don't want one?"

His eyes met mine. "I want yours." I let out a shaky breath, relieved. He went on. "But I'll admit, it terrifies me. Are you sure you do? Instead of spending your twenties having fun, going back to college, traveling? You'd be changing diapers and —shit, I know I shouldn't, but I still feel guilty that I claimed you so young. You had dreams..."

My eyes rolled so hard, they hurt. "Pax. I love babies. I've wanted my own for... forever. I mean, I wanted to work as well, but I can do both, right? We can juggle babies. Well, not literally. I mean, you could; you're so strong and muscley. But we'd have to have more than one to jugg—" He stopped my flustered babbling with a kiss, then rolled me so we faced each other.

"Let's talk babies. How many do you want, Candy?" He stroked my abdomen lightly, staring at it intently like it was some sort of crystal ball that might give an answer.

I wished I knew what the right answer was. He'd confided that he didn't resent raising his siblings, but had never thought about having his own family once they were grown. Would he really want to start over again?

"One would be okay. You've been down this road before. I know you're probably done with—hey! Why'd you spank me?"

He gave me an unrepentant grin. "I have never gone down this road, as you say, with my own mate. My own omega, my own children." He pulled me further up the bed, inserting his leg between mine. "And one is fine, if that's all you want. But true mates often have twins or even triplets. My mom had both. So you'd better get ready for some surprises, Candy Paxson."

I didn't know whether to laugh or cry, or both. "I want a lot, Pax. I want to have as many babies as we have room for in our house."

He blinked. "You know we have twelve bedrooms."

I shrugged. "We can build on if we need to."

"And you want to work, too?"

My heart felt like it was melting. "Maybe. I mean, we can afford a nanny, and I know a great service..."

A loud knock sounded at the door, and Lin's voice called

out, "Nicky?" Pax grabbed a robe and moved to the door, opening it a tiny crack. I could still hear her amused voice as she whispered, "Are you two done? It hasn't been a whole week, but you got quiet. Er, quieter."

"I think we could come out today."

"Thank goodness. Luke, Kati, and Teddy have to get back to work soon, and we have the family pictures, then a big dinner with Candy's guests."

"My guests?" I called out. "Mom and Dad?"

Lin laughed out loud. "Yes, your parents arrived a few days ago."

"Oh god, they heard all the elevator farts?" I stuffed a fist in my mouth, mortified.

"Elevator whats? Nicky, I think she still has heat-brain."

I crawled under the covers while Pax laughed. He came back to bed after a minute, interrupting my plans to move to a secret location and live out my life under an assumed identity. I would make a good surf instructor, if I learned to surf. Or an English teacher for really young kids in the Pacific. Or...

"You'd be great at all that. But if it helps, I'm pretty sure your parents have been staying at another one of our properties in Telluride all week."

"All week? They've been here the whole time?"

He stuck his head under the covers. "Sweetheart, of course they're here. Kati called them days ago. We were all so worried about you. You were lost on the slopes for hours in the snow. I promise I wasn't the only one terrified. Your parents wouldn't be anywhere else. They love you."

He whispered the next few words, like he wasn't certain what I'd say. "And I feel the same. I love you, Candy."

Chapter 24

Pax

I held my breath for a long moment, waiting for my little mate's response. I hadn't wanted to say those words for the first time when she was in the grip of her heat, or while I was knotting her.

I didn't want her to mistake what I meant.

"You do?"

I pulled her out from under the covers, wishing I could start over again with her, and wipe the uncertainty from her face. I'd made her feel insecure in our relationship, and it was time to fix that.

"I do, and even if I don't deserve you, I'm going to prove how grateful I am for the chance to spend our lives making it clear. Being your mate is my deepest dream come true. Every hope that someday I would have a love that changed who I am, made real." I took her hand and pressed it to my mate mark. "Can't you feel it, sweetheart?" I closed my eyes, concentrating on the emotions inside me.

"You do," she said at last, her voice filled with awe. And joy. "You really love me."

I cupped her chin on my hand. "Yes, and I will love you to the very end of my life, knowing you are the best part of it."

"I love you, too, Nicholas Paxson."

I felt the truth of that even before she said the words, but the soft statement sent another wave of joy through me. I pressed my lips to hers, and we both lost ourselves in the moment.

Until reality intruded, as it always does.

Lin called out our names, something hitting the floor right outside the room. "I'm leaving your outfits here, as well as Candy's purse and phone. It's lost its charge, sorry. You really do need to hurry things up."

"We have a charger here. Give us an hour."

Lin muttered something like, "Just don't knot her butt again."

Candy was a beautiful mess, her hair knotted almost as thoroughly as she had been. "No promises. Maybe make it two hours, sis."

I grabbed the box Lin had left along with some energy drinks, then ran back to the bed. Pressing a kiss on the top of Candy's head, I gave her closest butt cheek a smack, then strode to the bathroom. After a quick shower, I dragged my sleepy-eyed omega in behind me, washed and conditioned her hair, brushed it out, and blew it dry while her phone charged on the vanity.

I was putting a little smoothing gel on her hair when she said, "You're really good at this."

"I've had plenty of experience. Penny only stopped asking me to French braid hers three years ago." I winked. "I have some new fishtail braid patterns I've never tried. Didn't want to spoil her."

"If we have a daughter, you could do it on her." Her hand moved over her stomach, as if she were imagining it.

"To be honest, I can't wait," I admitted. "It's terrifying and exciting and wonderful, like being on that first hill of a roller coaster, thinking you might be carrying my baby. My babies." I dropped to my knees and turned her, so I was kneeling between her open legs. "I'm a worrier. But if it means getting to have you in my life, to love you? I'll learn to relax. Maybe I'll take up meditation and yoga, like Storm."

"Storm?" she asked, dragging her phone across the counter and turning it on. "Is he a friend of yours... *Oh, shit.*" She started typing as fast as her fingers could move. "Abort, abort," she muttered at the phone, scrolling through some texts, then dropping it with a groan.

"What?"

"Apparently, Rain flew in when I sent the code word. Your sister got her a room in a hotel across town. She'll be here in less than an hour."

"Good."

"No, Pax. Not good. You need to hide."

I laughed as Candy went on about pig farms and code words. But perhaps her heat had muddled her thinking.

"Seriously, Rain's going to be so pissed," Candy fretted as she did her makeup.

"I'll charm her," I said confidently. "She and I are going to be great friends."

Chapter 25

Candy

"I'm going to chop you into very small pieces, Mr. Paxson. And when I'm done, I am going to take those pieces, and chop them into smaller ones until I can't chop them any finer. And then I will take the tiny little pieces of you and put them in a box, and then I will blow. Up. The. Box. Do you understand me?"

I grabbed Rain's arm and pulled her away from Pax, who was doing his best not to cower behind the Christmas tree while she threatened him. She had burst in on the family picture a few moments before, brandishing a ski pole—only one —and demanding Pax lean over so she could "shove it up his ass and poke around to see if his head was still up there."

Pax's siblings were all watching my bestie with expressions that ranged from alarm to mild concern to vast amusement. What made it even more surreal was that every one of them— and me and Pax—were dressed in polar bear outfits.

I'd thought we'd be done with the pictures well before Rain arrived, but the men had almost staged a full-scale rebellion over the outfits. As it turned out, some of theirs had Velcro openings in the back, and peculiarly shaped "zipper pulls" that were almost the exact shape of a butt plug.

But after Lin had burst into tears over all the time she'd spent ordering everyone's sizes, they all got in line, smiled, and said cheese. Except baby Benjamin, who yelled, "Fuck!" every time the camera flash went off.

We'd just finished the final shot when Rain had arrived, trailed by concerned-looking security guards. She'd stormed in making a high-pitched pig call. "Soooieee!"

At least now she'd de-escalated to comprehensible death threats.

"He's apologized," I hissed, blocking her as she tried to grab the ski pole back from Luke, who'd confiscated it, but gotten a lump on his head in the process.

"That's not a bad pig call," Lin murmured, bouncing Benjamin on one hip. She didn't look too worried about Rain's behavior.

Vanessa grinned. "I'm not sure about the call, but I like her style. Alphas need to be kept in line."

"What was your name again?" Victor growled at Rain.

I smiled nervously at her, then him. I'd only just met him a few moments earlier, and I was pretty sure he thought I was all sorts of trouble.

Well, he wasn't wrong.

"This is Rain Torres, my best friend in the world." Probably second best after Soleil, but only because Soleil wasn't threatening to murder my fiancé. Though from her texts, she was on her way here as well. She'd arrived a few days before, and was staying with my parents across town. Thank goodness they weren't here yet.

"I'm her best friend, business partner, and ride or die bitch." Rain leaned around me to shout at Pax, "Which means you're going down, Paxson!"

One of his brothers muttered, "Pretty sure that's all he's been doing for the past five days." The others all agreed, and one of the sisters made a comment about the need for better soundproofing.

I shot them all a death glare. "If you don't know the fart in the elevator rule, I will let her loose."

"Is that omega a betasitter, too?" Penny asked, wide-eyed. She held her phone low in one hand, and I was pretty sure she was recording the whole thing. Apparently, Penny was a budding filmmaker.

I was pretty sure this would someday be part of a series titled *When Omegas Attack*.

Rain was quivering with not-so-repressed hostility. "Yes, I'm a betasitter," she spat out, wrenching free and marching up to Pax. She was only five feet tall, but I would swear he flinched. "But right now, I'm your worst nightmare, big shot. You hurt my best friend. I don't care if you're her true mate or not. She may have forgiven you, but there's nothing you can ever do to stop me hating you for what you put her through." She went up on tiptoes and whisper-shouted at his face, "I have the pig farm all picked out, you fucker. They'll eat your *bones*."

"Step away from my employer, ma'am," one of the security guards demanded. Rain just hissed at him.

"If you kill him, it'll hurt me, too, Rainy Day. True mates, remember?" I whispered, pulling her back again. Kati handed me a champagne flute. "Let's calm down and have a mimosa."

"You can live without a true mate," she muttered, but she took the mimosa. "I would know." She sipped resentfully, if that was possible. "This is fresh squeezed."

"And Dom Perignon." I nodded. "Have another."

She slammed it back and accepted a second one while the rest of the family backed away slowly. Kati murmured, "If the other friend is like this, we may need reinforcements," but didn't elaborate.

"You would know, you said," Victor said softly, handing Paloma to the nanny as he approached. "Rain Torres, we should talk."

She hiccupped. "Who the fuck are you?"

"I'm the new CEO of Paxson Pharma. I'd love to talk to you about... you."

She gave him the same look most women would give a guy who showed up at the door selling time shares or cheap solar panels. "The *new* CEO?"

I let out a breath. "I've been trying to tell you, Rain. Pax gave up his job. He's retired."

"Retired?"

"For good. For me."

She shuddered. "You're mated to a retiree. So. Old." I giggled, and she rolled her eyes as Victor chuckled in agreement. "Fine. You do anything else, Nicholas Paxson, hurt her in any way? I'll show you what an omega with nothing to lose will do." She glared at Pax for one moment more—pointing with two fingers at her eyes, then at him—before following Victor into the kitchen.

I peered around the room, taking in everyone's shock. "She's not normally this, um, homicidal. She's a great best friend, actually."

"Second best friend, you mean," a sweet voice came from behind me. "Wow. Are you all having a furry convention? Because I am on board with trying whatever kinky shit your new family's into, but I didn't bring the right outfit for this crowd. Oh my gosh, are those butt plug zipper pulls? I want one!"

Stunned, I burst into tears before falling into the arms of Soleil, who was standing in the doorway. "How did you get here? Why? When?" While I blubbered, everyone else started shucking off their costumes.

"I heard you needed your besties. Of course I came." She held up a bag, then handed it to Pax. "And I brought some pastries for your alpha! Nice to meet you, I suppose." Her smile was a little too bright.

I swiped the bag before Pax could get his hands on it, and shot her a look. "No poisoning alphas today, Soleil. It's all good now."

"Are you sure?" she whispered in my ear when I hugged her again. "And I didn't poison these. I just made them with an especially strong prune blend."

I blinked, looking around for the bag. One of the security guards now had it in his hand, and was glaring at it like it was a biohazard. Smart man.

"I'm sure," I told her. "No special pastries for my fiancé, Sun Bun. I'm keeping him."

"When's the wedding, then?" she chirped. "I don't see a ring. Anyway, your mom's on her way over in a limo, and if you don't have a date set, she said she's cutting off your alpha's balls with her sewing scissors."

"I'm so, so sorry... I lost my ring. It must have come off before my heat." I glanced up at Pax. "Your mother's ring. I don't know where it went."

He smiled and shook his head. "It doesn't matter. You're all I care about."

A chorus of "Awwwww" started up around the room.

For some reason, Luke approached. "It's okay, little sister. We realized it was missing and have had crews looking for it all week. They found it yesterday." He held up the ring, and Pax took it, thanking him. Then he grasped my hand and slid it back onto my finger.

"Candy, I love you. I want to marry you, and I promi—"

Pink-haired Penny interrupted with a scoff. "Aren't you going to get down on one knee? I'm so disappointed."

I peeked down at her hand. *Yep, still recording.*

Soleil whispered, "Your brother's very old, Pax's sister. If he gets down, he might not be able to get back up."

"I'm not that old!" he grumped, dropping to one knee. He took my hand in his again, taking a deep breath.

At that moment, Rain came out of the kitchen, yelling happy profanities when she spotted Soleil. She had an entire bottle of champagne in one hand. "This is the good shit, bitches. Let's get hammered."

"I might need some, in a minute." I stared down at my mate.

"Just a small glass for you," Paxson whispered, his gaze dropping to my abdomen.

"He still hasn't asked her?" Rain muttered to Soleil. "Think he's got performance anxiety?"

"I've heard old men get that a lot. But there's a pill." Soleil pulled her phone out of her purse. "I don't know what it's called. I'll look it up."

Pax closed his eyes and rubbed the bridge of his nose. "It's called Vialphren."

"Oh, you already take it?" she said cheerfully, putting her phone away. "Well, that's great! Maybe you just need a higher dosage."

Rain groaned. "Don't marry him, Candy. He already has to take pills to get it up; it's all downhill from here."

Pax's face was going a little bit purple. I was biting my lip as hard as I could not to laugh. "No, I don't take it. I *make* it. Our company... I don't need a pill," he finished while everyone laughed. "Can everyone shut up so I can propose?" He glared around the room, until they all went silent. "Candy Kane, will you do me the incredible honor of being not only my true mate, my future, and my reason to live, but also my bride? I want to spend every day with you, grow old with you—"

Someone muttered, "Too late."

Pax just laughed. "Will you?"

"I always thought making choices was hard. But this one isn't." I took his hand in mine, smiling so hard my cheeks hurt. His fuzzy polar bear ears flopped to one side, and his deep brown eyes gleamed with humor and hope.

The door opened again, and I heard my mom and dad call out, "Are we late?"

I rushed to get my answer out. "I choose you, Nicholas Paxson. Yes, I'll marry you. I'll marry you dressed up like a polar bear, if I have to."

"Oh, you're marrying a furry?" Dad grumbled as Mom grabbed me in a hug.

Mom stifled a laugh as she looked around the room. "A whole family of them."

Chapter 26

Candy

Five Weeks Later

We didn't get married in January. We were tying the knot at Paxson Lodge, with only my close friends and both of our families in attendance, on Valentine's Day. Pax had invited his friend Storm Halder, but Storm had gotten so sick he'd ended up staying in the hospital for almost the entire month. His doctor wouldn't clear him to travel.

We also weren't getting married in furry outfits. I'd seen Lin folding two fuzzy adult-sized onesies into a special case that had a side pocket filled with small lube packets and what I thought might be anal beads, though, so there was the outside chance we'd be dressed in fur on the honeymoon.

Soleil and Rain thought Lin's gift of a his-and-hers furry starter kit was weird, even though they both gave me equally inappropriate ones: a candy-cane striped double dildo, a set of nipple clamps with tiny peppermints hanging from them, and glow-in-the-dark grapefruit-flavored body paints.

But that was just the way omegas showed their love.

Or maybe that was sisters. I'd never had any, besides Rain and Soleil, who were the sisters of my heart. But I'd gained six grown ones in the past six weeks, and the first months of the new year had been a crash course in how to be part of a big family.

I loved having lots of siblings, and our family was going to keep growing. I rested a hand on the tiny bump that was almost totally hidden by my shapewear. We hadn't made an announcement yet, though everyone who would be here today already knew. How could they not, when Pax had turned into the biggest worrywart ever, hovering so much I almost wished he would go back to work.

Almost.

Penny had returned home with us, and her sisters had stayed a few nights at Pax's house—my house now, too—where we'd spent most of our evenings all together around the massive dining table, getting to know each other. I'd helped Penny with her homework, and she'd helped me learn how to use social media more effectively, although Pax almost lost it when he discovered she was a fairly influential influencer, even if all her videos were posted using custom filters, so her identity was safe so far. She hadn't used any of the video she'd taken of the family, though.

"That's just for us, Candy," she'd confided one night when we were tying candy canes onto a wreath for some of the wedding decorations. "Mom and Dad didn't do videos, and I grew up wishing I could hear their voices on more than their old answering machine messages. Life is uncertain, right? I want to make sure some of the most important moments are kept safe."

Even with only five weeks to do it, Kati had organized every detail of the ceremony and reception perfectly, including making sure all our family members and closest friends were there, ordering a cake, and even dressing her brothers in the same tuxedos Tom Hiddleston had worn on my favorite Pinterest board.

Valentine had been the biggest surprise. She'd taken my mom's old wedding dress—after I'd mustered the courage to tell her I didn't want to get married in nine yards of yellow hand-crocheted lace from the 80's—and asked for permission to make it into curtains and throw pillows for a baby nursery. Mom had been elated, and the two of them had spent hours sewing together.

Of course, that meant Kati had been free to find me the dress of my dreams.

In the bedroom where I'd had my surprise heat—now serving as the bridal dressing suite—Rain and Soleil helped me slip it on while Kati watched. The gown was a mermaid-style satin masterpiece, with swirls of blush pink circling the lace bodice and a pink and white beaded satin skirt.

"It's candy cane-colored," Rain muttered. "It's gorgeous."

She and Soleil had been swamped with requests for betasitters at Blue Skies, and we hadn't seen nearly enough of each other. In fact, this was the first time they'd seen the dress.

I jutted my chin out to stop the happy tears as she buttoned it up the back. "It's the one I fell in love with last year, from Sevartina's show. She only made one like it."

"Oh, yeah, we watched that online," Rain said as she finished the buttons.

Kati winked. "Sevvy owed me a solid."

Soleil choked out, "Wait. You're friends with Sevartina? The most exclusive designer for wedding dresses—for *any* dresses—in the world? The one who made the dresses for the last three royal European weddings, *that* Sevvy?" She pretended to faint.

Kati laughed. "I'll tell her you liked it."

While they chatted, I stared at myself in the mirror, at the way my dark, braided hair, woven through with rosebuds along with strings of pearls—and what I suspected were diamonds—made me look like the princess Pax liked to call me. "I swear, you're my fairy godmother, Kati."

Soleil mumbled, "Can she be mine, too?"

"You need a wedding planner?" Kati asked, perking up. "Do you have a special someone?"

"Eh, not really," she replied with a shrug.

"She has her own business," I interrupted.

"A slightly illegal one," Soleil said with a grin, "but yeah. It's hard for omegas to work above the table. Lots of us have to do pretty unsavory things to make ends meet." For some reason, Rain started choking on something, and went to grab some water.

"I'm glad I'm a beta. I love my job," Kati admitted, handing me a bouquet of pink, red, and white roses, with tiny candy canes interspersed among the blooms. "It's not as important as yours, though, Candy almost-Paxson."

I felt my cheeks heat. Even though Pax had stepped down as CEO, Victor had still given me a position at Paxson Pharma, and not as an intern. I was the VP of Global Philanthropy, a new spot created for whatever I wanted to build as part of the company's core values.

So far, we'd added Chilean maternity hospitals and vaccination clinics in Micronesia to our global focus, and expanded the Caritas food pantries locally. It had made my mom cry, and gone a long way to earning Pax her forgiveness.

"Isn't it time?" Rain asked, gathering up the smaller bridesmaids' bouquets.

"It is. You did an amazing job on the wedding, Kati," I said as Soleil took a last swallow of her hibiscus mimosa. "Thank you for everything."

"If I'd had another month, I could have done more. Sevvy said she'd love to put Nicky in a red and white striped tux." We both laughed while she adjusted the short train on my dress. "I'm so glad he found you. He waited so long, I thought he'd given up. But you're perfect for him. I'm so glad you'll be my sister." Rain and Soleil shooed her out before we all started crying and wrecked our makeup.

Alone, my girls each took a hand before Soleil sighed. "I'm sorry I wasn't here when you needed me in December."

"I'm sorry I won't be here in March. Blue Skies is going to be slammed."

Soleil's eyes twinkled. "I know. It's amazing how word is spreading."

"You're not sorry," Rain teased me. "You'll be in the Seychelles getting your baby bump rubbed with coconut oil."

"Among other parts," I agreed. "Pax just started a maternity massage course. Every single one has a happy ending."

"Aw, you're so pervertedly cute!" Soleil cooed.

Rain squeezed my hand. "Are you sure about him, Candy? Just because he's rich—heck, just because he's your true mate— that doesn't matter. You're sure he'll be good to you in the long run?"

I smiled into her dark eyes, then pressed my palm to my mate mark. "More than sure. I can feel him here. He's all in."

Soleil sighed. "Living the dream, Candy. I'm so happy for you."

"Better you than me," Rain mumbled, staring at my abdomen with a mixture of revulsion and fascination. "I can't imagine having kids."

"You two know how much I loved betasitting. Pax and I are going to have this baby, and probably more." I winked at them both. "And you'll be the first sitters I call when we need one."

"Remind me to change my number, Sunny," Rain murmured.

"Already on it," Soleil replied.

We left the bedroom laughing, but as I walked out into the main room of the lodge, with my two best friends on either side of me, and my parents standing in the circle with all of Pax's family, I couldn't keep a few tears from falling.

The room was decorated from floor to ceiling with fairy lights and vast swaths of white fabric printed with tiny candy canes. Electric candles had been placed on all the low tables, and the couches were all covered with soft, fluffy white blankets—an omega's dream. The air was thick with the scents of vanilla, cinnamon, lemon, pine, as well as my own strawberries and cream, and it made an almost intoxicating combination.

The happiness on the faces of all of Pax's family was staggering. They loved him so much, and now? They loved me, too.

Teddy cleared his throat. "Nicky, Candy? I invite you both to come forward and stand before your loved ones, and each other." His eyes gleamed as he looked up from the tablet where he had all our vows and the short service saved. He'd gotten ordained on the internet the month before, and had been incredibly touched that we'd asked him to perform our service. I'd caught him tearing up more than once at the short rehearsal the evening before.

Rain and Soleil let my hands go, stepping back as I reached my parents. Dad had tears standing in his eyes.

"My sweet girl," was all he could say before his voice broke. I hugged him tight, not caring if my gown wrinkled.

When he let me go, Mom cupped my face in both hands and whispered, "I'm so happy for you, my sweet Candy. And so glad you waited for the right alpha."

When I finally turned to Pax, I sighed at how perfect he looked. He wore a charcoal gray suit that outlined his muscular frame perfectly, and set off the salt and pepper at his temples. His mahogany hair swept low over one brow, and my fingers itched to push it back, to lose myself in his dark gaze.

His eyes gleamed with something like awe, but when he lifted his arm to take my hand, it was all I could do to keep from giggling. On his wrist sparkled a pinkish-red cufflink in the unmistakable shape of a grapefruit. Another gift from the girls, I assumed.

Teddy cleared his throat. "Dear friends, and family," he began. He read a poem by Rumi, and spoke about love and life-times, and how lucky we were to find each other in this wide world.

When he was done with everything but the vows, Lin whispered, "Time for the rings, baby."

Benjamin shouted at me from his father's arms. "Can Cay!"

When I nodded to his dad, he set Benjamin down, and the toddler waddled over to me, holding two small velvet boxes. I picked him up, ignoring the smear of sticky pink on his face as he gave me a smacking kiss on my cheek.

"Give them to Unky Nik-Nik and Aunt Candy," Lin encouraged. When he finally relinquished them, Pax took the smaller box, and I opened the larger one.

Inside was a platinum man's ring, etched with candies that matched mine, and inscribed on the inner band with four words: *I'll always choose you.* I slid it on Pax's finger. "I choose you, Pax, in the good times and the bad. I'll be here with you, taking care of you, and growing together."

His voice was raspy as he slid the band of pink diamonds onto my finger, where it nestled perfectly next to his mother's ring. "Candy, my love. No matter where you go, or what you want to do with your life, I will be there to support you. Every night. Every day. Through every decision you make—"

"*We* make," I interrupted, amazed I could even speak when my throat was thick with tears. "Pax, you're my choice. My alpha, and my love. We're going to love each other until the end of our lives."

"Maybe longer," he whispered.

And we did.

Epilogue

Candy

"Look, Candy, this will be perfect for Bon Bon," Lindyann cooed from the next aisle over at the Baby Boo-tique, a pop-up Halloween shop inside the "farmer's market" at the Westclear community. I gazed around the spacious, glass-domed enclosure, built to look like an enormous greenhouse, though no actual farming had ever taken place near here.

And the shoppers were certainly not farmers. Half the women in here I knew from the Omega League or charity functions—and it was all women, except for the security personnel, who stuck out like overgrown eggplants in a mini pumpkin patch.

Mmmm, pumpkin muffins. Pumpkin cake. Pumpkin cookies. I was getting hungry again, even though Pax had hand-fed me breakfast that morning. Well, if his cock counted as breakfast. Chef Adaline had followed that up with pumpkin pancakes, in honor of my last outing as a pregnant woman. I sucked in a deep breath of pumpkin-spice-flavored air, and tried to smile at my sister-in-law.

"First off, Lin, we're not naming the baby Bon Bon. I wouldn't do that to him. My parents gave me a hooker name, and I'm still working through my issues." I grabbed the hanger with the matching trio of black cat ears, paw coverings, and tails, in very obvious Daddy/Mommy/Baby sizes. "Second, Pax will never wear this. Not after he found out where you got the New Year's polar bear costumes."

Wrinkling her nose, she took the costumes back. "I didn't get *all* of them from Furry Emporium," she grumbled.

"Just give me a minute. I'll find something for the Halloween party." I needed a newborn baby costume, something loose for me postpartum, and something "dignified" for Pax. Finally, I found a long, peach princess gown. "I wonder if he'd think being Mario was dignified?"

"Pax? Try Bowser," Lin giggled. Her phone pinged. "Oof, that's Big Ben. Pickles needs to nurse again soon."

"I'll hurry," I promised. I felt a small twinge in my lower back as I leaned down to see a baby dino costume, and rested a hand on my belly. My security escort, Mickey, started to raise his phone to his ear, but I waved him off. "Just stretching."

I really did need to pick a costume fast. It was well into October, and the baby was twelve days overdue. My doctor had scheduled me to be induced tomorrow, and I knew this was my last chance to get out of the house before the baby came.

Our son. I sniffled, like I did every time I thought about a little boy with Pax's mahogany hair and chocolate-brown eyes.

I rubbed my eyes and glanced around the booth we were in. Ostensibly, it was a costume shop, but there was a whole row of Halloween-themed paddles on the back wall that had been decorated to read *Daddy's Bad Little Ghost* and things like that. I wandered toward that side of the stall. The nipple clamps with the little bats were so cute.

"I frickin' love bats," I mumbled, wishing my ginormaboobs were sexy enough to pull them off. Or at least less leaky. I picked them up anyway, remembering that morning's activities.

"*Wake up, sweetheart,*" *I crooned in Pax's ear.*

He groaned, rolling over on our huge mattress. "It can't be morning."

I stroked the short hairs at his temple. "Aww. Did I tire my old alpha out last night?"

Before I finished the last word, he had rolled over beside me and had his mouth on my neck, sucking at my mating bite. "I'll show you old alpha," he threatened.

"That was exactly what I was hoping for."

"How long have you been awake, sweetheart?" he asked, kissing his way down to my nipples. Pax was obsessed with my nipples, and they were equally as fixated on him. As my pregnancy had progressed, they'd grown more and more sensitive. I wasn't all that surprised. My boobs had always had minds of their own, especially my left one.

"Pax!" I cried out as his mouth closed over the nipple in question, and a bolt of pleasure shot straight to my clit, making me shudder in the early stages of a surprise climax.

Over the past few weeks, I'd started orgasming just from him playing with them, which was some sort of Holy Grail of sex, according to Rain and Soleil. I still preferred to have him inside me when I came, though.

"Pax," I whined once I'd come down from my peak, and he kept pinching and pulling at my nipples. "You'll make them leak."

"That's fair," he growled, his hands snaking down and opening my thighs almost roughly. "You make me leak." I reached for his thick cock and ran my finger over the top, where he was indeed dripping with pre-cum. I lifted my hand to my mouth, smiling.

"Yum. Breakfast."

"*Exactly,*" *he agreed, going back to my breasts, but letting his fingers draw slippery circles around my clit as well until I splintered into another firework of bliss.*

"*I'm still hungry,*" *I complained when I could speak again, and gestured for him to move up on the bed.*

"*You don't need to—*" *he began, then snapped his jaw shut when I snarled.*

"*Now.*"

"*At your service, my sweet wife.*"

I blushed, but didn't apologize. I'd gotten more and more demanding in the past few months, and even though everything ached—my hips, my back, my feet—his touch and his taste seemed to help regulate my moods and the discomfort.

I drew the tip of his cock into my mouth, wondering for an instant why this was the breakfast I wanted most in the world. But then his salt and musk hit the back of my throat, and the omega in me took over, drawing him deeper, my tongue moving around the top half of his length, and one hand, now slicked up with my own juices, wrapped around the bottom and resting on his knot.

He hadn't been able to knot me in the last month of my pregnancy. Not that the doctor had recommended against it; in fact, she'd mentioned at my last check-in that late-stage knotting was a good way to bring on labor. Pax had agreed to try it at some point, but he was nervous that he'd hurt the baby.

That ends today. I smiled around his cock as he groaned, and sucked harder. I'd tried to bring on my labor by doing all the regular things: eating spicy foods, taking long walks, even eating pineapple. But I had a feeling what I really needed was my alpha's knot.

And I was going to take what I needed.

I cupped his balls, feeling them begin to tighten as his climax approached, only to find myself being maneuvered around until his mouth was on my core. He held off, and I barreled closer to my peak, until I whined again. "I want to come with you inside me, Pax."

"You're the boss," he teased, taking one more long lick before he pulled away. "How do you want to do this?"

I stared down at my enormous belly. The baby was being quiet for now, though I had a feeling he'd start kicking my bladder soon enough. "Me on top?" I asked, trying not to let him see what I had planned. I moved slowly until I was balanced over him, sitting upright. As I sank down onto him, he held me protectively, keeping me balanced, and I relaxed. In only a few short thrusts, I was at the brink again.

And so was Pax. "Now?" he grunted. "I don't know if I can wait..."

"Then don't." I pulled away from him, lifting myself just high enough. I could feel his climax beginning to move through him, and I knew this was my moment. I was slippery with my own release and his pre-cum, and when I let myself down again, my weight and the momentum had his knot sliding inside me before he could react.

His eyes flew wide, as his knot instantly swelled and locked into place. "Brat!" he managed to say before he let out a shout of pleasure and his warmth filled me.

"Your brat," I panted as I ground down on him, feeling one more orgasm at the edge, then letting it cascade over me in a series of waves.

I'd had a few cramps since then, and the baby had been squirming around. But no real labor pains, just the regular Braxton-Hicks contractions. I set down the nipple clamps and turned, spying a rack I hadn't seen from the front of the shop. It was a Goldilocks set, with a Daddy Bear, Mommy Bear, and Baby Bear costume that came with a tiny Goldilocks doll.

It was perfect. I pulled the Mommy Bear ears on and

turned to find Lin. "Look," I called, when I suddenly felt a gush of liquid on my inner thigh.

And then heard it splash on the floor.

"Lindyann?" I squeaked. "I think it's time!"

In seconds, my sister-in-law had the costumes in her hands, Mickey had me on his arm heading for the car, and I had Pax on the phone.

"Meet me at the hospital, Daddy Bear," I panted out, as a small contraction rippled through me. "We're going to have a baby."

Epilogue

Pax

"We're going to have a baby." I repeated the words to my laboring wife, as if this was news to her, and held an ice chip on a spoon up to her mouth. I felt helpless, idiotic, like I was spitting on the flames of Hell to make a dent in her pain.

Why had I not insisted we live in the hospital for the last few weeks? If she'd already been here, in our family's suite, she would have been able to get the epidural in time, before she was too far dilated. Watching her suffer was the worst agony I had ever endured. I would give anything to help her. But all I was allowed to do was feed her ice, and soothe her.

"Candy, princess, we're going to have a baby."

Candy took a break from her breathing pattern to shoot me the dirtiest look I'd ever received. "Who's... we... asshole?" she managed to say, then screamed.

The nurse who was examining Candy's dilation perked her head up. "Looks like it's time to bring in Dr. Grantham." She paused. "Again." Now she gave me a dirty look. "Do you remember what you promised?"

"No growling at the doctor."

"And?" she prompted.

"No threatening to sue the hospital."

"Or...?"

"Or ruin her financially, for making my princess suffer."

"Okay, I'll be right back. Don't push just yet, Mrs. Paxson." The nurse pulled the edge of Candy's gown back down, then left the room.

Left the room? Fuck! I lunged for the door, but Candy's whimpers had me back at her side. "Sweetheart, what can I do?" I could see from the monitor that the contractions were starting to come one on top of the other, but she still managed to smile blearily at me.

"I love you," she whispered. I pushed the sweaty tendrils of her hair back and smiled down at her. I could feel the tears dripping down my face, but they didn't matter. Only she did.

"I love you, too. My perfect mate, my strong, beautiful wife. I love you more than I'll ever be able to show you. But I'm going to spend my life trying."

"I like... your ears," she gritted out, another contraction ramping up. I adjusted the costume ears I'd forgotten about. Lin had stuck them on my head when I arrived, saying they were a present from Candy.

"I'll never take them off," I promised.

Her nose wrinkled. "Too far."

"I'd do anything for you, my love. Anything. I'm so proud of you. So proud to be by your side." I kissed her forehead and stared into her flushed, sweaty face.

"Pax... we're gonna have a baby," she panted. The monitors were beeping, the graph on it ramping up again.

"I know, angel, I know. As soon as the doctor comes back—"

"No!" she shouted. "NOW!" She hunched forward,

bearing down, and I threw the gown back. A head capped with dark hair was already showing.

Where the *fuck* was that doctor?

Candy screamed again, and I moved as fast as I could to the end of the table, yelling for the doctor, or the nurse, or *anyone*. Behind me, the door slammed open, and the room filled with qualified medical experts. I almost passed out with relief.

"My, my. Looks like your son is almost here," the completely useless doctor said as she moved me to the side with one hand. Then she ignored me—as she damned well should—and coached Candy for the next few moments.

I watched in awe and wept as my son was born. I stared in wonder and wept some more when the nurse showed him to me. When the doctor offered me the scissors to cut the umbilical cord, I took them with shaking hands. Then I stood by patiently as the medical staff cleaned up the room and gave instructions, while the nurse laid the baby on Candy's chest.

The nurse's voice seemed to come from a long way away, as I took in the miracle before me. "We'll be back to do the normal tests and measurements. But you three take a moment first. Say hello."

Candy's dark eyes were red-rimmed as she smiled at me. "Come here." I perched on the edge of the bed, unable to look away. "Breathe, Pax. You look like you're going to pass out."

I'd stopped breathing? Yes. Yes, I had.

"He's perfect," I said once I'd followed her instructions. She nodded, tucking a finger inside his impossible small fist. "What's his name?" We'd both agreed to wait until the baby was born to decide. I had a list of three names.

Candy had a list of thirty.

She chewed at her lip. "How many middle names can we give him?"

"Two," I said with a grin. "So you get three choices. And

nothing weird. None of that Jason spelled J-a-e-z-u-n-n nonsense."

She rolled her eyes at me. "You're such an old fart."

"Brat," I teased, pressing my lips on the baby's head, then on her lips, in a soft, slow kiss. "You can choose three names."

"For now," she agreed. "Three for you, and then three for the next. And three for all the little Paxsons who come after."

"So you don't want to choose?" I asked, half-amused, and half-stunned. "Together, we picked out thirty-three names."

"Eleven babies too many for you, gramps?"

I blanched. "Eleven pregnancies. I... I can't..." The baby let out a little cry, and began rooting around for her nipple.

"Not necessarily eleven." Her dark eyes twinkled as she peeked up at me. "Twins and triplets, remember?"

"If that's your choice," I managed to say, though hysterical laughter threatened. "I'll give you anything you want. Whatever you choose."

With a smile, she whispered, "I choose it all. As long as it's with you."

Thank you for reading! I hope you had fun getting to know Candy and Pax. Could you please leave a quick review? Indie authors rely on these to help our books find their readers, and I appreciate these more than I can express.

If you haven't read Soleil's story in Sunshine's Grump, it takes place a few months after Knotty New Year. Valentine's Heart and Rainbow's Storm are next!

Acknowledgments

I owe a huge debt of gratitude to my beta readers who comforted me with positive messages, memes, Henry Cavill pics, and more than one round of "emergency" reads as I spun this tiny knotty tale into a whole-ass novel just in time for the holidays.

Grapefruit-sized thanks to Editor-Dominatrix Raewyn Ash, Author Sarah "Double Fist" Reynolds, and Courtney "Stop Crying Merri" Betabirch for the tough love.

My deepest, girthiest gratitude goes out (and all the way in) to the Perfect Pink Posse: Miranda May, Jacquie, Kristin, Alex, Bekka, Kelliann, Lorna, Renee, and Megan.

Thank you to my ARC readers for waiting patiently, Darcy Bennett for keeping me from going too far off the rails, Kate at Y'all That Graphic for the fantastic new covers, and the amazing Mr. Bright for pouring the cinnamon tea.

Also by Merri Bright

The Spy's Solstice

Roya's Story:

The Assassin's Promise

Wren's Story:

The Leviathan's Debt

The Wyvern's Redemption

Ratter's Story:

The Goddess's Spy

About the Author

Merri Bright spends her days dreaming up naughty angels, misunderstood demons, sexy shifters, growly Alpha males, and frequently refuses to limit her heroines to just one love interest.

Please join Merri's Mischief Makers on Facebook where you'll discover random giveaways, sneak peeks of new novels, book recommendations, and silly/sexy/funny stuff. Or email her at merri@merribright.com.